Ashley Undone

Mickey Hadick

PARKSIDE BOOKS
HOLT, MICHIGAN

This story is dedicated to my parents,
whose influence guided me long after
they left this world, whether or not I
realized it at the time.

What profit hath a man of all his labour which he taketh under the sun?

Ecclesiastes 1, Verse 3

MICHIGAN

Marquette
Sault Ste. Marie
Escanaba
Beaver Island
St. Ignace
Alpena
Traverse City
Bad Axe
Mt. Pleasant
Muskegon
Flint
Grand Haven
Grand Rapids
Lansing
Holland
Royal Oak
South Haven
Detroit
Ann Arbor
Kalamazoo
Monroe

Ashley Undone

Mickey Hadick

1

ASHLEY

BEFORE MY MOM DIED, BEFORE I even knew she was sick, I once asked her what happens to us when we're dead. I asked if we become like ghosts, or are we like angels, and if there was a heaven.

She laughed. "Of all the bedtime questions, that's the hardest question of all."

"Why?"

"Because we can't really know for sure. We can believe something, or wait and find out."

I told her that sounded scary. "What do you believe?"

She took a deep breath. "It's not going to be like it is now, when we're living. It'll be different, but I don't think it'll be bad."

"It won't be like the bad place?" I remember snuggling in close to her, whimpering a little. She wrapped me in her arms and kissed my head. She smelled like grass, which I recognized from lying out in the backyard with her on warm days, enjoying the sunshine.

"We don't know where we were before being born,"

she said, "and we made it here okay. I think it'll be like that."

"That scares me."

She hummed a little tune into my hair. "I know it doesn't sound good, but it's part of life. So it'll be okay."

"I'm scared you'll die and no one will take care of me."

She gave me an extra squeeze and a kiss. "That's not going to happen. But even if it does, Daddy loves you as much as I do. He'll take good care of you."

"Promise you'll watch over me if you can."

"I promise. You're my little girl. I promise you'll always feel my love, even when you're a big girl."

She hugged me and tickled me, which was a fun, if sneaky, way to change the subject. I went to sleep after that.

Then she got sick and died.

Fast forward eight years and I felt alone, lost, and maybe even like I was in the bad place. My dad had remarried and this new "mom" was kind of a bitch.

My dad was more interested in his business and his new wife than he was interested in taking care of me. I hated living with them, so I moved out on my own; I felt lonely, but I didn't want to move back. Everything sucked.

On one of my visits to my mom's grave, I told her about Dad's latest idea for me.

"He wants me to go work at Britney's new coffee shop," I said. Britney was my step-sister, but we had hardly talked in eight years. "It would suck to work for Britney, but Dad really wants me to do it. I don't even like coffee. I'm guessing he thinks working for Britney would teach me to love money as much as he does."

There was no one else at the cemetery; just me, the overgrown grass, and all kinds of birds flapping all over the place.

Then it got real quiet, and I thought maybe I'd get an answer. I heard my mom's voice speak softly into my ear like her head was right above mine, whispering so only I could hear.

She said, "Take the job."

Britney and I had nothing in common. She's older, was popular in school, and won a state championship in tennis. I, on the other hand, watched a lot of TV shows and avoided people. I swear she forgot I even existed half the time. Maybe as her wage slave she'd finally pay attention to me.

Obviously, my dad just wanted me to do something, so I didn't worry him, and he could focus on making money.

Sophie—my stepmother—bought the coffee shop and gifted it to Britney, which was on-brand for Sophie, using money to manipulate other people.

When Britney put me in charge of the coffee shop, I think it was to annoy Sophie.

Still, I was proud of how I managed the place, leading the baristas, managing vendors, and dealing with customers. I had nothing on my mom's engineering skills or my dad's entrepreneurial savvy, but I could make a kick-ass cup of coffee.

One day, Britney came into the coffee shop with a we-have-a-problem look on her face. While I made her a drink, she bit down on her lips. She wanted to say something, but there were customers—two men in their thirties—within earshot.

She motioned for me to join her at the table in the front. As I made my way around the counter, I noticed both those men studying Britney's ass.

Britney was wearing a blouse and skirt combo. Her hair was in a ponytail, which gave her neck and cheekbones a chance to dance in the light. The four-inch heels made her calf muscles pop.

No one ever watched me walk. I dressed frumpy, prioritizing comfort.

"What's the matter?" I asked.

Britney caught the men looking. She turned away and frowned, but also stole a glance at her reflection in her phone screen, checking her teeth for lipstick. "A couple of things," she said. "Not sure where to begin."

"Start with the good news if the bad news is funny."

"Profits are down," Britney said, frowning at her macchiato's bitter bite. She crossed her legs at the knee and jiggled her foot, dangling the shoe from her toes. The two men cast glances, mesmerized by her foot's arch, or a twitch in her calf, or I don't know what.

I slid two packets of sugar across the table. "That's the good news? There's no way you'll have something funny for the bad news."

"Stop being weird," she said. "None of this is funny.

This is a business and businesses are supposed to grow and make money."

"Business seems the same."

"Seems? Aren't you tracking it?"

"Nope."

Britney stirred the sugar into her drink. "I think you should start."

"People come, they buy coffee, then they go. Sometimes they buy a bagel or a sandwich."

"Didn't you take any business classes at community college?"

I shook my head. "Shouldn't you have asked me these questions before hiring me?"

"Don't be an ass. I'm serious about the profits."

"Does it matter how profitable we are? Profit is profit. That's good, right?"

She took a binder out of her bag and flipped to a page with a chart on it. "I compared our business operation to industry benchmarks. Our output per barista is below national average."

I laughed. "When you opened this place, we had twice the number of employees. Now I'm the manager and you pay me the same. Everybody here works plenty hard. No customer waits more than a couple of minutes for their drink."

"You're not getting it," she said. "If it's not profitable enough, there's no point in running a business."

"Fine. Raise the prices."

She put the tiny cup down hard on the table. "That's even worse. There's a drive-through Biggby at one end of the street and a Starbucks at the other. We're in the loser bracket and we can't have any unforced errors."

"Did you get that metaphor from your business professor or your tennis coach?"

Britney folded her arms. "Do I need to bring Quentin back to manage?"

I laughed again. Quentin had been her boyfriend when the shop opened. Quentin was a fine name for a coffee shop manager, but not someone Britney slept with. "You're the boss," I said. "Do what you want."

"I want you to fire a barista," she said, lowering her voice. She flipped through the papers in her binder and took out a sheet of paper, and waved it at me. "Joan's getting too many hours."

The paper she waved was my "Joan log." Britney let me bring on a friend, but only if we paid her in cash off the books. I tracked Joan's hours in a spiral-bound notebook, paid her cash out of the register, and tore out the sheet of paper at the end of the month so Britney could balance the accounts.

The thing was, Joan was actually me. Whenever I worked alone, I'd reward myself with extra cash, but I didn't want to simply skim from the register. I invented Joan as an on-call employee. Rather, she was the idea of an employee.

I gave Britney my most serious look. "Joan's my friend."

Britney tapped her fingers in rhythm with her jiggling foot. "She works really random hours."

"That's what I like about her," I said. "Someone calls in sick and Joan is always available."

"You have too many baristas. If somebody calls in

sick, make do without."

"I can't handle this place alone. I need Joan."

"We're not profitable enough."

"We're not profitable enough for what?" I asked.

Britney closed the binder. "We're not profitable enough to be attractive."

"Are you looking for a suitor?"

"I'm thinking about it."

"Then maybe we should change the sign out front to a picture of your ass."

Her nostrils flared, which pleased me. I motioned toward the two men seated across the café. Britney caught one of them looking. He smiled.

Britney smiled back.

A customer came in and I left Britney to take the order. I could have let the other barista take the order, but I wanted Britney to see me being busy.

Obviously, it would be simple enough to stop "paying" Joan and continue working, but there was a principle at stake. I wasn't just going to fire my friend to increase profits, even if she didn't exist.

I understood the need for a business to make money, but not the need for profit to be more important than people. More to the point, I understood that greed drove people with money to think differently. Soon, they only cared about the money. That's what had happened to my father.

When I returned to her table, Britney said, "Listen, I'm just really stuck. I'm not loving this small business ownership thing, okay? It's a lot of paperwork for not a lot of money. I'm ready to dump it, but Sophie will be pissed, because, well, you know…"

I said, "If you're expecting me to treat my baristas like animals just so you don't have to confront Sophie about the shop's profitability, it ain't going to happen."

"There's another way. You could buy it."

"Buy what?"

"Buy the business."

"Why would I want to buy this business? Profits are down."

"I need you to be serious," she said. "Sophie thinks Dad will give you the money."

"Wait," I said. "You don't want to tell Sophie you want out, but you asked her about Dad giving me the money?"

"I spun it as an opportunity for you to do something with your life. I said I think you're ready."

My fists clenched, and I leaned forward. "I'll decide what I do with my life."

Britney pretended to ignore me and checked her teeth for lipstick again with her phone.

I took a breath. "I don't want Dad's money. Look what happened to you when you took Sophie's money."

"I'm fine with taking Sophie's money," she said. "I didn't ask to be her kid, so I'm not going to feel guilty about being born into a wealthy family."

"That's nice for you, I guess, but I don't want to be some bourgeoisie business owner."

"Think of it as controlling the means of production."

"Touché."

"So you'll consider it?"

"Look at me," I said. I wore thrift shop clothes. My sneakers were in tatters. I hadn't paid for a haircut in my life. "I like serving people coffee, but I hate taking their money. You think I want to own this fucking place?"

Britney folded up her binder and crossed her arms. Lowering her voice, she said, "Yes, you do. Otherwise, I'm selling to some piece of shit who isn't going to put up with your friend Joan working weird hours all week. And for cash, by the way. You can't pay people under the table. What if she gets hurt? She won't be covered by insurance."

"I promise you, Joan is not going to be a problem."

"The next owner will run this place like an actual business that turns a decent profit, which is what I would do if I could get you to act like an actual manager."

"Do what you have to do," I said, "but I'm not taking my father's money."

Britney stood up and shoved the binder into her shoulder bag. "Whatever. I hope you think about it quick, because I've already been contacted by an interior designer looking for a showcase location. You and your baristas will be out of work, and people from Ypsilanti will be shopping for high-end wallpaper and lamps. You want the gentrification to end? You want to keep this quirky coffee shop open for the late-night hipster crowd? Figure out how to turn more profit with coffee."

I thought she was about to leave, so I grabbed her wrist. "What's the bad news?"

"Oh fuck," she said and flopped back down in the

chair.

# # # #

BRITNEY HANDED ME HER MAC AIR. "IT'S infected with something."

I paused, waiting for the punchline. "You sure?"

"Turn it on," she said. "You'll see."

"RansomWare?"

"I guess. They want Bitcoin or something."

I set the computer down gently, like it might break.

"What?" she said. "Why are you making that face?"

"It's pretty rare. What were you doing?"

She reached for it. "Never mind. I'll take it to the Apple Store. That'll be less embarrassing."

"I'm sorry," I said. "It's a legit question. Knowing how you got infected may help fix it."

She sat down again. "I was trying to do the right thing. I clicked on a stupid ad for a utility to protect it against viruses or whatever."

"Did you install something?"

"Yes."

"Okay. Now I know."

"Can you fix it?"

"I'll try."

She took another sip of her macchiato. "Thank you."

"Were you on a porn site?"

Britney set down her cup and stared. "I was shopping for shoes."

"So 'yes.'"

During the quiet time at the coffee shop, I turned on Britney's laptop and noted the RansomWare demand, which read: "You have been Klobbered. Your files are encrypted, but don't worry. Transfer 0.2 Bitcoin and all will be restored…" Yada-yada.

It went on about assurances for future protection and included a link to transfer the Bitcoin.

I had never heard about this, but Google had. Within a few minutes, I read several articles about this attack. I came upon an article by a security researcher who detailed how to remove the infection and decrypt the files.

This attack was a few years old. It wasn't particularly clever, relying on the utter lack of operating system skills of most Mac users. The Mac OS spoils them, and most don't know how to use a command line or deal with actual files.

Not that there's anything wrong with being that type of user. It just makes you more vulnerable to this attack.

I scrounged a thumb drive, set it up as a bootable drive, installed the software needed, and inserted it into Britney's Mac Air. A few minutes later, the software was plodding through the file folders, decrypting each file.

I thought again about what Britney had suggested. My heart raced and my breathing sped up. The mere thought of taking money from my father was upsetting.

I stood up and paced across the room. What would

people say about me, cashing in on my father's success? What would my mother think about me?

She'd be disappointed, for sure. Would she be angry? Would I be failing her by not helping my dad keep his promise?

Maybe working at the coffee shop *with* my father would be okay with my mom.

I felt a little nauseous and drank some water, then went to the bathroom in case I vomited.

Why was this falling to me to figure out? I was barely an adult. Unlike with Britney's laptop, I couldn't google how to fix this.

This was also my mother's birthday, and I was supposed to meet my father at her grave. I waited just inside the cemetery entrance where I had a view of the dirt road leading to the bridge over Lake Ringerton. Ten minutes after our arranged time, he still hadn't arrived.

I called his cell phone but his secretary answered, which confused me but really wasn't a surprise. "Where is my father?" I asked.

"Sorry, Ashley," Cassie said. "He's stuck in a meeting and I don't think he can make it."

"Is that like being stuck in quicksand?"

"I'm sure he'll call as soon as he can," she said. Her tone was conciliatory and gentle. She was practiced at this.

"Don't bother," I said and hung up quickly so she wouldn't hear me cry.

Back at my place, while I waited for Britney to come pick up her Mac, I busied myself with topping off the bird feeders in the backyard. The weeds were taking over the lawn and crowding out the planting beds behind the house and around the garage, but I went around admiring them. I was renting, so it was not my problem. And besides, I wasn't sure it was a problem. Weeds deserve to live and most of them are pretty interesting.

Britney found me out back and held up her Mac Air for me to see. "You should lock your front door. I waltzed right in and there it was, on the coffee table."

"Sorry," I said. "But I don't think there are any thieves around here."

"Don't be naïve."

"Don't be paranoid."

She shook her head. "Listen, I'm grateful you fixed it. I didn't mean to pick a fight."

"It's okay."

"Let me give you some money."

"No," I shrilled. "I didn't do it for money." My fists had clenched and my shoulders were tight. I scared myself at how angry I'd gotten, so I folded my arms and took several deep breaths.

Britney raised her head as if about to complain—something I recognized from the coffee shop—but she sighed and lowered her head, looking at me with her face downcast. "You're right," she said. "I'm just really grateful. I felt stupid, and I was convinced I'd lost everything. I thought money would show you how much I appreciate what you did."

"It's fine. I shouldn't have snapped, but I'm your stepsister, not the valet parking attendant."

"Yeah, well, you did save me money I would have spent at the Apple Store."

"Give it to an unhoused person."

She scrunched up her face like she stubbed her toe.

"Fine," I said. "Don't give the money to an unhoused person. Buy yourself a pair of shoes."

The mention of shoes relaxed her because she looked around at the yard. "What is going on out here? Do you need so many bird feeders?"

"I think the birds are happy," I said.

"You like looking at them, or what?"

"Sometimes I talk to them." Of course, she seemed incredulous, but I pressed on. "When they sing, they're talking to us. So I talk back. They're kind of my friends."

"Ashley…"

"It's fine. They aren't my only friends, but I really think they know me. I care about them and they might just care about me."

Britney hugged her laptop and patted it. "So maybe I'll bring some seed for your friends in gratitude."

"That'd be great."

She got serious. "I talked to Dad. He's definitely interested in helping you get the coffee shop."

Then I laughed. "You really didn't listen to me, did you?"

2

After Britney left, I drove straight to my mom's grave and told her what happened. "Britney only wants me to buy the business so she can use the money for something else, but I'm afraid of what will become of me if I take the money from Dad. I'll only care about profit and loss. I'll see the staff as numbers on a report. I'm afraid I'll become what you didn't want me to become. I'll become like Dad."

It was a rant, but that's how I talked to my mom now that she was dead. I got everything out because I wasn't sure what she knew. Did her spirit roam the world, or was she stuck right there? I'd only connected with her at the grave, so I assumed she was stuck there. I had to give her everything about the situation.

Talking about it helped relieve my anxiety and stress. I sat down on the grass and watched a cloud pass in front of the sun. It was June, close to the solstice, and there were still a few hours left in the day. The warmth felt like a hug.

My mother didn't speak to me per se, at least not in

conversation. Sometimes it was a feeling that came over me. Other times, an idea would pop into my head. And I'd occasionally hear her voice. I always recognized when it was from her spirit. I had to calm myself and be ready to accept it, however she gifted me with the answer.

As I waited, a blue bird landed nearby and stole away with the stem of a leaf from the lawn. It flew to a nearby elm and waited.

I got up and walked under the elm. As I approached, the bluebird flew to the edge of the cemetery and into a bird house. It ducked inside the little hole, then popped its head out. We made eye contact before it flew away.

Someone had planted the birdhouses, each with a pitched roof overhanging the single hole, along the border of the cemetery. Beyond the rusted iron fence, fifty feet of tall grass gave way to tall reeds and pussy willows at the water's edge. Beyond that was Lake Ringerton, tranquil in the light breeze.

The cemetery was on a small peninsula, jutting out into the water. The dirt road at the entrance went off into a wooded area in one direction and, in the other direction, a bridge to Ringerton. The air was heavy with the scent of water, algae, and earth just then. One of our regular family walks used to be out to that cemetery. My mother enjoyed the scent of the lake and always mentioned how she liked living by water.

As I returned to my mother's grave, the answer I needed came to me and I knew it was what she would have wanted.

# # # #

I DROVE TO MANSIONVILLE, THE LOOP OF massive houses north of Ann Arbor on the shore of the pond. It's a strip of land incorporated as its own township, but it's more like Luxembourg, a tiny place where rich people move to live near other rich people. No one buys a house without thorough vetting.

The only regular people in Mansionville are me and the service staff. My dented Honda Civic, covered in a layer of grime and bird droppings, was probably the cheapest vehicle in a three-mile radius.

My father's house was one of the few without a gate —Sophie's only concession. The rest of it—the driveway forming a circle in front of the house, the three-car garage on one side, a carriage house on the other, and the eight-thousand square foot single family residence in the middle—was all Sophie.

The house was a big-ass colonial with dormers and columns, like something you'd see in a movie. Almost all the houses were big-ass colonials. A few, wishing to stand out, were like Tudor manors.

The door was up a flight of stairs, making the front of the house imposing. I let myself in—I used the electronic code to unlock the door—but waited in the atrium. "Dad?"

Twelve feet above me was a raised walkway connecting the second story of the two wings. Sophie, dressed in a red skirt and cream blouse, appeared on the left side. "Oh, it's you," she said. Her eyes narrowed and her lips pursed. Her eyebrows knit slightly, but her forehead was smooth as ice thanks to Botox. But I already knew she didn't like me.

"I'm looking for my father."

She held her glasses in one hand and raised them slowly to her eyes. "So I heard you shout."

She set the eyeglasses on top of her head, pushing back her dark hair, which she kept short and done up in waves. I had to admire how this woman in her late forties kept herself faithfully committed to the look of a woman of means. Her skin was smooth and her cheeks were prominent. There was no jowly sag along the jawline. Her eyes had a hint of feline shape, the only giveaway that she'd had work done.

"Is my dad here?"

"His office," Sophie said. "But take those filthy shoes off."

I slipped off my Birkenstocks and realized my feet were dirtier than the shoes. Sorry, Sophie. I walked down the hall without glancing up at her.

"Oh," my dad said. "Hey Sweetheart." He was at his desk and turned off his computer monitor and closed his laptop, like I'd caught him looking at porn.

"Do you need some time?"

"It's fine," he said. He frowned. Whispering, he said, "Close the door."

That was a little weird. "Are you sure you're okay?" I whispered back.

He nodded. "I'm going over the finances at the company. Profits are down and I'm trying to figure it out."

"It must be contagious."

He shook his head in confusion.

"Anyway," I said, "I think you should give all the profits to the employees."

He scoffed. "Is that what you came here to tell me?"

"I need a favor. Kind of a big one."

"Let's hear it." He stood up and drew a small handgun out of a holster behind his back, placing the gun on his desk.

"Christ," I said. I backed away from the desk. "Why do you have that?"

He seemed to have no idea why I'd be concerned. "I've had this for years."

"But why?"

He bent down and took a box out of a desk drawer. That turned out to be a gun box, with another handgun in it, just like the gun on the desk. "I'm worth a lot of money. You can't be too careful."

I was sick to my stomach. I hate guns as much as I hate capitalism. The thing I hate more is the idea you have to defend capitalism with guns.

He put the gun in the box, put the box in his desk, and locked the desk. "It's safe, Sweetheart. You can relax."

"No, I can't."

"You have nothing to worry about."

"Can we talk somewhere else?"

A look of contempt passed over his face like a shadow. Had I blinked, I'd have missed it.

We went out back to the patio. It's like an outdoor living room with columns and a trellis roof, two all-weather sofas, a grill and a wet bar. On a warm summer evening, even I have to admit it's like paradise because of the trees and the lawn sloping down to the pond. A breeze swayed the canvas sun shades strung between the columns.

He handed me a glass of water. "What's the favor?"

I told him about Britney and the coffee shop, and wrapped up my request as positively as I could. "But if you bought the coffee shop, and kept me on to manage it, we could work together on something. Then maybe you could leave the business, like you promised Mom, and spend more time with me."

My dad closed his eyes and nodded, smiling slightly. His face was relaxed, almost youthful. He had dark hair—still no gray—and always seemed to have the shadow of a beard started. His normal way to look at you was with a wide-eyed stare, which could be misunderstood as creepy if you didn't realize he was giving you his full attention. With his eyes closed, he seemed approachable, like this was just an average guy who would listen to your problems. And I swear that's how he was, how I remember him when I was little, before my mother died. But ever since he'd gotten with Sophie, that attentive stare was a poker face as he calculated his play.

He offered a tight-lipped smile. "I don't know a thing about the coffee shop business."

"I could teach you."

He laughed and shook his head, his eyes glancing at the far corner of the room.

"What?" I said. "You think I'm stupid?"

"Not at all."

"Then why did you make that face?"

He waved his hands as if nothing was wrong. "It's just that I really love what I'm doing now."

"You're just making money. How much do you need?"

"It's not like that, Sweetheart. Besides, I can help a lot of people with this kind of money. You know that."

"I know you promised Mom to give the company to the employees. That would help them a lot."

He groaned. "I don't think it was to give away the company. That doesn't make any business sense. Besides, if I gave it to them, they might not take care of it."

"Holy shit, Dad, they're not toddlers. They're professionals who sacrificed their lives to make the company work, and Mom thought they deserved to have a secure financial future because of that."

He drummed his fingers on his seat cushion. "It's a little more complicated than that." He shook his head again and puffed out one of his cheeks.

"You think I'm being stupid again?" I asked.

"No, I don't."

"You keep making that face."

He waved one hand in a circle beside his head. "It's just that I have a weird money problem with the business right now that's really baffling me."

"Whatever." I hurried back into the house to get to the front door. It was rude and churlish, but I didn't want to have the type of discussion we had four years ago, before I left the house. I grabbed my Birkenstocks and scampered down the front steps.

He caught up with me as I opened the Civic's door.

"Come on, Ashley. Let's talk about it."

"If you don't buy it, Britney is going to fire my best friend, Joan. If Joan quits, she's going to have to go somewhere else to work, probably Detroit. Maybe Philadelphia. I'm going to go with her."

"Philadelphia?"

"Joan talks about Philadelphia a lot because of the music scene."

"Okay," he said. "I don't understand that part."

Obviously, I was improvising the Joan stuff to convince him. "It would mean a lot to me if we could work together on this, owning a coffee shop, even if you're still not quite ready to honor the promise you made to Mom."

He sat on the top step with his arms propped up by his knees. "Hang on. One thing at a time."

I sat down behind the wheel but didn't close the door.

He got up from the steps. "How about if I give you the money to buy the coffee shop?"

"I don't want to own the means of production," I said. "Remember? I want to destroy capitalism and the patriarchy."

"How about if I get one of my friends to take the business off of Britney's hands? I'll make sure Joan can keep her job."

"You seriously have no interest in working with me at the coffee shop?"

He held his hands up like he was apologizing. "I really don't, sweetheart. I'm too old to learn something new, and I really love my work. Why don't you come work with me?"

I closed the car door and shouted, "You made a promise."

He motioned for me to roll down the window. "Things changed once your mother passed on."

"Yeah. You slept with Sophie."

"I fell in love again," he said. "That's not unusual. You know, we both lost our spouse. That's part of the attraction."

"Sure it is."

"Sweetheart, don't be like that."

I noticed Sophie watching us from the upstairs window. Even with the reflection of the trees in the window, I could see her scowling at me. Her nostrils flared and her lips pulled slightly to one side. She didn't blink, and it was pretty creepy.

It occurred to me that the ransomware which humbled Britney earlier might remind my father that his business could end one day whether he liked it or not, just as Mom died despite all the money spent to get her the best doctors.

Of course, it would be pretty awful of me to infect his company with ransomware. I didn't think I could do it. But Joan…Joan could do it.

"Would you give Joan a job?" I asked.

"Where?"

"Your company."

"Doing what?"

"We took some IT courses at community college. She's good with computers."

"I think we're always looking for people to do

technical support."

"So you'll hire her?"

"Sure. Email me a resume, and I'll send it over to Frank."

I started the car.

"What about the coffee shop?" he asked.

I put on my seatbelt to stall for a moment, not quite sure what to say. "Only if you run it with me."

3

As I drove out of Mansionville, Kirsten popped into my head. I had to go see her.

Despite renting a place not that far from mine in Depot Town, I hadn't seen her in almost a year. I'd been so busy at the coffee shop, and had sunk into a kind of self-pitying funk living alone, that I hadn't made the effort. It was all my fault because Kirsten invited me to go tubing on the Huron with her and her roommates last summer, and again on the first warm weekend of May. She'd invited me to their Halloween party, and their New Year's Eve party, and to build a snowman.

I was embarrassed at how lame I'd become, but also knew it was because I'd gotten pissed at my dad. Instead of dealing with him, I punished myself by staying alone.

Kirsten squealed with joy when she opened the door and hugged me, pulling me inside. We sat on the sofa, pushing Todd, one of her roommates, aside.

He'd been watching a cartoon—The Fairly Oddparents—and I was transfixed. I hadn't seen it in years and couldn't think of why I didn't watch it myself.

Kirsten tugged on my arm. "What's going on?"

"I might have a problem."

She pointed at Todd. "Do we need privacy?"

We didn't. I knew Todd would not be a problem.

"I asked my dad to give Joan a job at his company," I said.

"Joan Naumov? She's back?"

"No," I said. "The other Joan."

"You?"

"Yeah."

"As Joan?"

"Yep."

She made faces: confused, then bemused, and finally amused. "Oh. Okay."

"What?"

"Nothing," she said. "I didn't think you were still doing that."

When I suggested to my dad that he hire Joan, I thought of me-as-Joan as being another person. You probably don't believe me, but that's the only way I can think to explain it. That's why I didn't feel guilty about paying Joan under the table for helping at the coffee shop: Joan, in those moments, is not me.

I didn't think of it as a split personality, but as a dominant persona, the way people act differently at fancy events if they're dressed up. Like when people go to a renaissance festival in costume, they act like they're in the Renaissance. Probably the only time people are their true self is when they wear pajamas and slippers to shop at Target for Motrin and tampons.

Maybe I wasn't *actually* Joan when I dressed as "Joan," but I sure wasn't Ashley either.

"I hadn't been doing Joan lately," I said, "but I have to now."

"Did you get fired from your sister's coffee shop?"

I explained that situation, and how I used Joan, at least on paper, to get extra money.

"That's cool," Kirsten said. "But wouldn't your dad just hire you?"

"There's something I may need to do, but I can't do it as me. Only Joan can do it."

"Can you handle being Joan again?"

I took off my glasses and pulled my mop of hair back. "I think it's my only way to get through to my father."

Kirsten took a big breath. "You want me to help you?"

"Yes. I need help with the hair."

"You still have the wig?" she asked.

"Yeah, and most of the clothes and also the driver's license."

Kirsten stood up. "I'll get the clippers and we'll send Todd and Julie out for some hair color."

4

JOAN

I was scheduled for an interview with the CFO, a guy named Frank, who "Ashley" had heard about a few times from her father. Frank, apparently, was in charge of I.T. Not that it makes any sense to put technology under the CFO guy, unless he's just a bossy prick there to bully the people who do the work.

I dressed to show what I've got: hair was short and red, a low flame but throwing heat; four studs along the rim of each ear; enough cleavage to hold my phone for a hands-free call.

Most guys would think I want something sexual. Most guys are idiots. That day, I wanted the job.

I knew I could handle computer stuff. Ashley was smart enough but mostly didn't care. But Joan liked a challenge and liked attention. Also, Joan could get the nerds to help her at the school's computer lab a lot faster than Ashley.

But I was going for this job because Ashley couldn't do what I was going to do. Ashley would get a simple job to learn the business. Joan could get her hands on the computer servers running the business.

HD Enterprises was a smallish company, but pretty big for Ringerton, so I assumed people dressed up a bit. I arrived for my interview dressed for success: a cherry-red, above-the-knees sheath dress that showed my curves. My black shoes had five-inch heels.

The security guard—Vince, according to his name tag—got up from his desk to hold the door for me.

I realized I'd forgotten to bring one of those little leather-bound notebooks people take to interviews. Vince offered me his own notebook, complete with "HD Enterprises" embossed on the leather. When I held out my hand to accept, he wrote his name and number on the top sheet in case I wanted to reach him. Classy.

Some skinny-faced guy in his mid-twenties named Jared came down to the lobby to get me. He had dark hair, a sharp jaw and brown eyes. A classic frat boy now living the dream, a cloud of smug floating above his head.

He kept a straight face, but as we got into the elevator he grinned. "What do you think we do here?" he asked.

"Excuse me?"

"If you dressed for the job you want, I'm just curious what you think we do here?"

He wore a suit coat and dress shirt open at the collar, like he shopped in the CEO section of the Halloween store.

I didn't take the bait. He seemed very pleased with himself and didn't need any encouragement to be an asshole.

Luckily, it was a quick ride to the third floor. There

were only a handful of offices up there and a smattering of desks in the middle. Modern, abstract art was displayed on the walls between the windows. It was quiet. The air felt about sixty-eight degrees, like ice on my neck and chest. As we approached Frank's corner office, there was a view of trees and the pond on the eastern side of the building.

The morning light poured into the waiting area beside the secretary's desk. As I passed it, the aroma of leather from the sofa warming in the sunshine reminded me of the furniture at Mansionville and took me out of my head as Joan. I felt out of place—like Ashley when Dad first took me to the new house.

I (Ashley) had a moment of panic that someone there in the office would recognize me as the boss's kid. But Joan wouldn't give a shit. Joan would laugh it off.

Jared winked at the secretary as he escorted me into this Frank's office. He actually winked. The secretary, I was happy to see, stared back at him, unmoved.

Frank sat at his desk and glanced at me, but focused on Jared. He waved and pointed. "Close the door on your way out."

Jared shot a glance at me but didn't seem perturbed.

Frank introduced himself, rising from the desk and extending his paw. "I'm Frank Marshall." He was over six feet, barrel chested, and had a jaw like an anvil. He was somewhere in his forties and had all of his hair; possibly, he had a little of someone else's hair to boot.

"Joan Naumov."

"That a Russian name?"

"Are there Russians here in Ringerton? I thought we

were all Americans."

Frank smirked, his eyes flitting up and down as he checked me out. He nodded to the chair and settled into his over-sized throne, the cushion exhaling like a whale's spout. "So you're a friend of David Rice?"

"I'm friends with his daughter, Ashley."

Frank nodded slowly. "You're an expert with computers?"

"Expertise is relative."

"Is that supposed to convince me?"

"I know a few things about computers, and they don't intimidate me."

Frank leaned forward. "I bet they don't."

I scribbled in my notebook like I was jotting down a note.

"And you want to work here?"

I scribbled a little more. "Sure do."

"You got a resume or something?"

"You could look at my LinkedIn profile, or see my portfolio at joan-naumov-dot-com." That was a website I'd pulled together the night before, copying stuff from other websites and pasting it onto mine.

Frank put his hands on his computer keyboard, then pulled them back. "Fuck it."

Before he could say anything else, the office door opened and a young woman—older than me but maybe still in her late twenties—came in. She was pregnant, wore a dark blue, contoured dress and she wore it well.

"Sorry, Frank," she said, holding up a stack of papers by way of explanation.

Frank waved her in and she came around the desk. "Nikki Watkins, this is, uh…"

"Joan Naumov."

"Thank you," Frank said.

Ms. Watkins offered her hand coldly, not trying to get too friendly. She had long, brown hair coiled over her shoulders, and a wide mouth painted a dull shade of red. Her nose was long and her forehead seemed big enough to install an LED display. She had brown eyes and carefully contoured eyebrows.

"You'll be joining us?" Nikki asked, glancing at my breasts.

"I hope so."

While Frank signed a form, Nikki crossed her arms. "I didn't realize we had any openings at the moment."

"We don't," Frank said. "But I.T. always needs help."

"Where'd you go to school?" she asked.

"I'm attending Washtenaw Community College."

Nikki frowned and turned toward Frank.

"She's a friend of David's," Frank said.

"Actually, I'm a friend of Ashley."

Nikki studied me, her eyebrows knitting together. "Who is Ashley?"

"David's kid," Frank said.

The eyebrows raised up. "Did you get that dress at Nordstrom Rack?"

"Nordstroms at Somerset."

She made a point of looking at my shoes. I was wearing Jimmy Choo.

"Are you sure you need a job?"

Frank was watching with passing interest. "You going

to check her underwear?"

"I'm guessing she hasn't any," Nikki said.

"Hanes," I said. "Got them at Target."

"See that?" Frank said. "She's sensible. Perfect fit for our team: showy on the outside, but all business inside."

"Maybe don't try so hard," Nikki said. "I mean, you're already the CEO's friend, right?"

"Thank you, Nikki," Frank said. "I'll talk to you later."

Nikki shot him a look before she left and I realized they probably had a thing going, which might explain why she gave me grief.

Frank leaned back in his chair. "It's a nice dress. You look good. Great, in fact."

"Thanks."

"So how do you know Ashley?"

"School. And I work with her at the coffee shop."

Frank smiled. "I bet you're one hell of a barista."

"It's coffee," I said. "I fill cups and leave them on the counter for people to drink."

A moment passed as he contemplated what to say next. There weren't any pictures of family in his office. A couple of golf trophies, some of those dumb executive gift toys on his desk, and a picture of his car. *His car.*

It was just a hunch about him and Nikki, but you see it in people who meet at the coffee shop. Even in Depot Town, I saw one of these couples about once a week: an older, tall, boss-like guy with a younger, good-looking woman dressed for the office. It's supposed to be an innocent cup of coffee, then you notice they're trying too hard, and it's actually a date in the middle of the afternoon.

"Jared should be waiting outside."

I got up to leave.

"Thanks for stopping by," he said. "I enjoyed seeing you."

5

Jared called to offer me the position as I was driving home. "Can you be there at nine?"

"In the morning?"

"Yes," Jared said. "We start at eight but I need to arrange some things, first."

"Sure."

"I thought coffee shops open early."

"I'm not an opener."

"So eight won't be a problem, from now on?"

"Probably not."

"You don't sound too excited," Jared said.

"Sorry. I appreciate it."

"Swell. Be here at nine. Ask for Brian."

"Does Brian have a last name?"

"Sassy. Great. I'm sure that gets you lots of tips at the coffee shop."

"So everybody knows who Brian is?"

"The security guy will know," Jared said. "Cool?"

"What does it pay?"

"What do you make as a barista?"

"Not a lot."

"This will pay more than that."

Maybe I shouldn't have asked because the money wasn't the point. I was taking the job for a good reason but it wasn't my career. I didn't even want the money. Money messes people up. I was fine with whatever I had.

I know that's a bullshit thing to say. The world runs on money. The only reason I didn't really need more was because I (we) inherited some.

I wanted to go talk to Kirsten, but she would be at work for a few hours. I drove around Ypsi, cruising in the Honda Civic. At an intersection near Eastern, two guys —frat boys, most likely—driving a Mustang convertible, checked me out. "Ready to party?" the guy in the passenger seat called out.

When I glanced over, the driver revved the engine. "Where *are* you going?" the other guy asked, and they both laughed. They were laughing at *me*.

I couldn't think of a comeback. I just wanted to ignore them and raised the window, realizing it was because of the Honda Civic. The Civic was Ashley's car. I was dressed as Joan but felt like Ashley when I sat in this car.

I drove back towards the highway to that stretch of Michigan Avenue lined with car dealerships and bought a car. I bought Joan a car. I decided Joan would drive a Dodge Charger with an enormous engine.

Here, of course, is where I have to make a confession.

That inheritance I received from my mother, which was given to me when I turned 18, was more than enough for a brand new car. In fact, I bought a used car—the Ashley in me hates to buy new things when used is just as good. I paid for it with the debit card from the credit union.

The credit union called to confirm the transaction, which reminded me that Joan would need her own phone and probably a couple of other things to go along with the driver's license.

In for a penny, in for a pound of flesh, as someone once said.

Ashley hated the idea of buying a car, but Joan put on a show. The car salesman stared at my cleavage right until I took out the debit card. Once the purchase was approved, and my insurance agent faxed over the proof, the salesman stared at the cleavage again.

It got worse because I wasn't trading in the Civic. The salesman offered to follow me home and give me a ride back to the dealership. I drove to Kristen's neighborhood, instead, because I mostly didn't want this creep to know where I lived.

We had a moment because he got out and held the passenger door open for me, like I was going to let him drive my car with me in the passenger seat. I held out my hand for the keys and he was confused.

"If you want to walk back to the dealership, that's fine, but you're done driving my car."

I still felt sick during the drive back because the guy's cologne was stinking up the car. The steering wheel felt dirty because he touched it. I figured he was the kind of guy that would fart at will, and that's why he used so much cologne. I promised myself I'd give the car away when all of this was over.

When, at last, I returned to Kirsten's in the new Charger, she was amazed.

"You like it?" I asked. "You can have it in a month."

"Must be nice," she said. Her head tilted back slightly, and I felt resentment.

"I'm sorry," I said. "I know you must hate me, but it's not my fault. I need to do this thing. I swear I'm not trying to show off."

"Okay," she said. "I didn't say anything."

"But you looked like you hated me."

"I don't, Ash, I promise."

"And you can seriously have the car," I said. "I won't be Joan forever."

I had stepped away from her and folded my arms to cover my boobs. I wished I had the wig to cover my head, suddenly desperate to be Ashley and to be left alone.

"It's really okay," she said as she hugged me. "I want to help you, but are you sure you know what you're doing?"

"I'm trying to do an Ocean's 11 thing."

"The movie?" she asked.

"I think I can get my dad to keep his promise, but I have to get ahead of him so he can see what's at stake."

"You're kind of fighting the patriarchy," Kirsten said. "Like Thelma and Louise."

That shut me up for a minute or two, and Kirsten waited while I stewed. "The problem with Thelma and Louise," I said, "is that they had no leverage. Danny

Ocean always has leverage."

"The problem," Kirsten said, "is that we haven't even seen those movies. We watch YouTube clips, or hear about them from comedians or on sitcoms."

She had a point. I wasn't even sure how that movie ended. "I'm not saying this is fool-proof, but I can't think of another way. I've waited too long already."

Kirsten took my hand. "You can just come live with us. We can be your family. It's okay to do that, to choose who is in your life rather than fighting to hang onto someone who has moved on."

"I know, but I really want to try this."

She took a deep breath. "What can I do to help?"

"I get computers," I said, "but how do I dress like someone who gets computers?"

"You want to dress like a nerd?"

"Yes!"

She pulled away and nodded towards the house. "Let's go raid Todd's closet."

I showed up the next day and met Vince the security guy at the front door.

"Congratulations," Vince said. "I heard you're local. That's good because it's like family here."

"Some families suck," I said. It was a joke, and Vince got it.

"It ain't as good as before, but it ain't bad."

"Before what?"

"Before the boss's wife died."

The lobby was a large space, high-ceilinged, like an

atrium. The waiting area was nicely appointed, with two sofas, magazines, and a mini-fridge filled with water bottles. I flipped through a magazine and caught up on celebrity gossip as I waited.

A pasty guy approached. "I'm Brian," he said. "I think I'm your boss."

He was average height but above-average size. I don't think he left his desk very much because he was puffing. This was his workout for the day. His hair looked like he trimmed it himself. It was nine o'clock and he had sweat stains under his arms.

Our first stop was the coffee station, where he topped off his mug and shook in a thick layer of creamer powder. I couldn't help but stare as he swirled it into a semi-liquid the color and consistency of chicken gravy.

"You sure you don't want some?"

I explained how I had previously been a barista and started each day with some high octane coffee. "I'm fully amped, but thanks."

"I have to admit," Brian said, "this is unusual for me. I was only told you were coming this morning, and that I should find something for you to do."

"Oh, well, thanks for doing this, then."

"When the boss's nephew tells you to make work for the CEO's friend, you figure it out."

"I'm not the CEO's friend," I said. "I'm the CEO's daughter's friend."

Brian shot me a look, and we both left it alone.

Next we went up a floor to the finance department where we worked out some things with Genie and Colleen, who, together, were the entire Accounts

Payable team. Brian introduced me by saying some stuff about my working there on a service contract, which I didn't understand.

"This is highly irregular," Genie said. "We rarely do service contracts with individuals."

"It's usually with a company," Colleen said. "Then they send us people."

"Do you have your own company?" Genie asked.

"I don't know what you're talking about," I said. "I thought I was getting a job."

"Didn't Jared explain?" Brian asked me. He settled himself into a chair and asked Genie to call Jared.

"We're bringing you on with a service contract," Brian said. "If it goes well, we might create a position to hire you full time. It really shouldn't matter to you."

"Will I get benefits, like medical?" I really didn't care, but that seemed like something I should ask.

"No," Brian said. "But do you have that now?"

"No."

"At least you're not losing anything."

"Fine. Whatever."

"But we still don't do service contracts with individuals," Colleen said.

"Why does that matter?"

"We just don't do it," Genie said.

Jared arrived. "Nice outfit," he said and winked at me.

I tried to hide my annoyance. I was wearing khaki slacks and a polo shirt, trying to look like the guys on the IT team. Thanks to Kirsten's roommate, who dressed like Brian, my outfit was kind of perfect.

Brian, still out-of-breath, caught Jared up about the situation.

"Here's what you do," Jared said. "Hop on the Secretary of State website and create an LLC for yourself. Then go to Horizon Bank and open an account for the bank—it's free to open an account. Bring the account number back here, and Genie the Meanie and her friend Colleeny will get your paperwork taken care of."

"Wouldn't it be easier to hire me as an employee?"

"We don't just hire people because they're the friend of the CEO," Jared said.

"Jared," I said, "aren't you the nephew of the CFO?"

Genie and Colleen laughed.

From the look on Jared's face, he didn't like the joke. Brian had said it a few minutes earlier, and I probably pissed him off for repeating it. I really shouldn't have made that joke.

About two hours later, Brian met me once again at the front lobby and escorted me to Accounts Payable. I gave Genie the information for my LLC business account, and she filled in the blanks on a contract.

"We still need legal to approve," Genie said. "But it's almost time for lunch. Maybe we should wait until this afternoon."

"Please ask the legal team to come down here," Brian said. "I can't have this hanging over me any longer."

Colleen got on the horn, Brian wandered off to top off his coffee, and I was offered a seat at an empty desk.

When I bumped the desk, the mouse moved and woke up the computer. On the screen was an accounting general ledger system.

"You use QuickBooks?" I asked.

"Yeah," Genie said. "Do you know it?"

"I know of it," I said. "I'm more about using computers, not accounting systems."

"Well, we need that," Colleen said. "You'll do great."

It seemed my joke on Jared had earned me an ally.

Jared showed up. It turned out he was the legal team.

He handed me a set of typed pages stapled together. "Here's the Master Service Agreement. It gives us the right to end this agreement, without notice, and to sue you for damages."

I flipped through the pages. I had seen nothing like it before, but I had nothing to lose, really, and I had to sign it to go forward with our plan. So I signed it.

Jared offered it to Genie. "Can you notarize this?"

Genie hesitated a millisecond before getting her notary public stuff out of the drawer. She stamped it and signed it and embossed it.

"Do you need to see my identification?" I asked.

"I'm not one of those notaries," Genie said.

Jared handed the signed document to Colleen. "Make a copy for Joan and have the original sent up to my office."

Jared offered me a thin smile. "I guess you can get to work, and we'll see you back here tomorrow at eight."

"Since I'm not an employee, does it matter what my hours are?"

Jared rolled his eyes. "Work it out with Brian because,

honestly, I don't care."

At some point Brian had wandered back and was sitting at a nearby desk, flipping through his phone. "She good to go?" he asked.

"You understand how to get paid?" Genie asked.

"Nope." I mean, of course I didn't understand, but I didn't want to insult Genie the Meanie.

She waved a few more pieces of paper around. "Fill out these time sheets, have Brian sign them, get them to us."

"I can do that."

"Then we transfer money to your LLC bank account," Genie said.

"Like taking money from a baby," Colleen added.

Brian's team was slightly more organized than the juggernaut of efficiency that legal and accounts payable formed. But it wasn't without its flaws.

First I met Edna, the secretary. She went by Eddie, thank God. Edna is a terrible name. In middle school, they probably called her Gonadna, which doesn't rhyme, but middle school kids are assholes that way.

She had pictures of her two kids plastered all over the cubicle, and her coffee mug had "No Coffee, No Workee" printed on it.

"Thank you," she said. "Another woman. I'm sick of these nerdy guys."

"Don't listen to her," Brian said. "She loves us."

Edna-Eddie had sandy-blonde hair, a wide face, and bags under her eyes. She was pretty and smiled generously. She wore a "Life is Good" T-shirt and Target jeans.

"These guys don't even bowl," Eddie said. "Do you bowl?"

"I used to," I said. "But my mother died in a bowling accident, so…"

"Oh, my God. I'm so sorry."

"I'm kidding."

"Oh you bitch," Eddie said, and fell back in her chair laughing.

The next three cubicles gave us Mike, Pat, and Oscar. I was told that Mike handled the network and the file servers, Pat managed the Windows configurations, and Oscar was the Active Directory admin and the firewall guy. Each one was critical to keeping the computers working.

"Do those guys have backups?" I asked. "Or don't you ever let them take a day off of work?"

"They back each other up," Brian said. "And Ingrid knows enough of everything to be dangerous."

Ingrid was in a room where they prepped new laptops or workstations, installed stuff, and set the employees up with the equipment. She was also the help desk and trained new users.

"That's a lot of everything," I said.

"Keeps me busy."

I liked her. She seemed easy-going and had a system figured out with shelves for computer components, a testing station, and a place to take phone calls when people needed help.

"So, what's she doing here?" Ingrid asked. From her

tone, it seemed she didn't like me.

"Joan will help you," Brian said.

"Help me what? Go to the bathroom?"

"Help you with whatever. You complain about having too much to do. Have her do some of it."

"I have a system," Ingrid said. "I don't want her messing it up."

"Figure it out," Brian said.

"It will take longer to teach her how than to just keep doing it myself."

"She's a friend of the CEO, so…"

"So I have to babysit."

"Yes."

"Fuck me."

"Hey," Brian said. "Language."

"*Trakni menya*," Ingrid said, which I think is Russian.

"Anything else?" Brian asked. His coffee cup was a little low, and I think he was itching to top it off.

"Where's she sitting?"

"Cubicle next to yours."

"Great."

"I'm going to get some coffee," Brian said. "Call me if you have questions."

Brian left and Ingrid, staring at her monitor, shook her head. I looked around a little more carefully.

There were half a dozen boxes from HP stacked in the corner by the door. Probably new laptops. Next to the stack was a bunch of broken down cardboard boxes and Styrofoam packing material. A long workbench had three laptops at one end and a couple of others spaced out along it.

On the back wall was shelving, with bins for parts and components. They were labeled "Hard Drives," "Memory," "Hubs," and "Mouses." The sort of stuff you need when you fix or upgrade computers.

The other wall had another long workbench with monitors spaced along it.

Overall, it had a total computer lab vibe, and Ingrid didn't look like she wanted to share the space.

"You want me to take out the trash or recycling?"

She looked at me like I was crazy. "That's figured out, okay? On Friday, the cleaning crew comes and gets it. You telling me that looks like shit? That's on you. Everything in here is right where it needs to be."

"Sorry."

"Tell you what," Ingrid said. "I'm giving you the best laptop we got, and you can sit your ass in a cubicle and fuck with it until I figure out what you can do to help me."

"Fine."

She went to the first workbench and grabbed one of the stacked up laptops. "This was for one of the engineers, but he can wait another day."

Ingrid handed me the laptop then grabbed a charger, Ethernet cable, and mouse from the bins.

I made a beeline for Eddie. She'd been friendly, and I needed help.

"Where's Ingrid?" she asked.

"She seemed pretty busy. Too busy, I guess, to set me up."

"Fiddle sticks," Eddie said. "We're never that busy. Let's get you settled."

She re-introduced me to the three guys: Oscar, Pat and Mike. "Ingrid is too busy," she said with heavy sarcasm.

"It's because she never learns keyboard shortcuts," Oscar said.

"Ingrid should have the easiest job here," Mike said, "but she makes it the hardest."

"She won't use scripts," Pat said.

"I'm a fan of Powershell," I said. "But I love Python."

Oscar nodded. "A Pythonista. That's my girl."

"She just gave me the laptop," I said. "I'm going to need a login."

Oscar waved me into his cubicle and built my profile in Active Directory. "It's first name dot last name at H·D·E·N·T dot com."

"Password?"

"Password with a little p, then you get prompted to create a new one."

I sat in the empty cubicle and fired up the laptop. A couple of minutes later, I was on their network and thanked Oscar for the help.

"I mirrored Ingrid's profile for yours, so anything she can do, you can do."

Mike stepped into my cubicle and handed me a diagram of computer boxes. "That's our server farm," he said. "The engineering team has their own servers, but we still maintain them. But if they break one, they have to fix it."

"Not your circus, not your monkeys."

"Exactly," Mike said. "But we help them if they get stuck, obviously."

"Obviously."

The laptop went through a series of software installs and operating system patches. In between logins, I looked in the desk drawers. A few paper clips, pencils, and a server diagram similar to what Mike had given me. Nothing I didn't already know.

Ingrid appeared in my cubicle. "I saw you on the network," she said.

I nodded.

She handed me a mouse and a power adapter for a laptop. "Take this to Thomas in Engineering."

I hesitated, expecting her to explain how to find Thomas in Engineering.

"It's not all glamorous," she said. "You have to do the shitty stuff."

Edna, offering me directions, pointed across the floor. "The engineers are even bigger nerds than theses guys," she said. "You can't miss 'em."

I meandered across through the cubicles, pausing at the empties to glance at the computer monitors and the documents scattered across the desks. Security was lax: computers weren't locked. Technical drawings, project plans, and financial statements were left abandoned.

Thomas was a skinny guy with glasses and a short-sleeved dress shirt, which he buttoned to his neck. He blushed when I stepped into his cubicle.

I offered the mouse and power adapter. "You wanted these, right?"

He nodded. He handed me a large, heavy laptop in exchange. "I guess you can take this boat anchor back to the lab."

"Will do."

And just like that, I had pretty much everything I needed to bring down the company. There was still the matter of the admin password needed to install software on all the computers and servers, but maybe that wasn't strictly necessary.

Soon, I could advance the plan to destroy my father's company.

6

DAVID

DAVID WAS AT HIS DESK ON the third floor, struggling with the cash flow enigma plaguing the company, when Sophie, his wife, barged in.

"Don't mind me, Darling," she said.

David scowled as she crossed to the windows on the other side of the office. She looked outside, never at David, so his annoyance was for naught.

"She does have a certain something about her," Sophie said.

"Who's that?"

"Oh, you know, the little treat you had Frank hire for you."

"Excuse me?" David went to the window.

In the parking lot, Joan's red hair drew the eye. She wore a golf shirt and khaki slacks, but on her, those simple articles of clothing looked different than on anyone else.

Sophie raised her eyeglasses and smiled at David. "Nikki complained about her. I wonder why that is."

"What did Nikki say?"

The sound of the Dodge Charger starting pulled their attention back to the parking lot. The engine revved wildly, *dangerously*, David thought, before pulling away at high speed and roaring out of the parking lot.

"It's not so much what Nikki said as what she implied."

David sighed and leaned against the windowsill. "Please, just fucking tell me so I can get back to my work."

Sophie walked back across the office to close the door. She sat on the sofa and crossed one leg over the other. "I don't appreciate the tone, darling. I'm your wife and an officer of this company. Neither one deserves the vulgarity." She picked up the remote control and turned on the television. It was tuned to a financial news station but muted.

David sat in the easy chair across from the sofa. "I'm sorry."

"Don't worry about it," Sophie said, her eyes watching the television. "As for Nikki, she said, 'I hope this one can do a little bit of work, otherwise it's pretty clear why she's been hired.' She told me I can see for myself if I looked outside."

"And what, exactly, do you think she's implying?"

"That you hired this Joan to boost your ego."

"I don't think I've even met Joan."

"She's telling everyone she's a friend of yours."

David scoffed, launching spittle onto his hands folded in his lap. "It's a favor to Ashley. I think it's the kid she hung out with when we lived here in town."

Sophie turned off the television. "Well, that's a relief."

"Great. I'm going to get back to my work."

"So you won't be home right away?"

David settled into his chair and scanned his desk and his computer monitor, trying to gauge the work. He found his pen and tried to pick up his thoughts.

"Darling? How long?"

"Couple of hours?"

"I'll see what Marta was planning for dinner, and maybe we can eat at eight."

"Sounds good."

"Britney is coming over later to discuss something, so be home no later than eight."

David, annoyed, dropped his pen on the notebook. "What's going on?"

"I said, 'something,' so if I knew more, I'd have said that."

"Probably about money, then?"

"Probably. Yes."

"Money is a problem right now," David said, and waved a hand at his desk.

"Whatever you think is a money problem is probably not that bad."

"Maybe it's just an issue, rather than a problem."

Sophie lowered her glasses to the tip of her nose. "If you'd listened to Frank two years ago, and pursued going public, or finding an equity partner with deep pockets, our money issues would be gone for the rest of our life. We'd all have money to burn."

"I'm not surrendering my company simply for money."

"I'm not in the mood for this discussion." Sophie

stood and straightened her skirt. "I'm meeting Frank for tennis and drinks. Care to join us?"

David was amused. "Won't three be a crowd?"

She smiled back at him. "Not at all. It's a chance to talk shop and relax. At least join us for drinks. I promise he won't bring up private equity or going public."

"Where at?"

"Our house, of course."

"I'll try to wrap this up a little early."

"I'll ask Frank what he thinks of this Joan."

David smiled. "Maybe she's more his type than Nikki is."

Sophie faced him from the door. "What do you mean to imply with that?"

"Oh, I don't know," David said. "I thought I heard someone say he had a thing for Nikki."

"Who told you that?"

David thought a moment, trying to connect his comment with the source. "I thought I heard it from you."

Sophie raised her eyebrows. "Well, if I said something like that, it probably meant nothing."

7

ASHLEY

I was alone, closing the coffee shop, when Britney came in. She sat at her table in the front and scrolled her phone while I finished what I was doing.

"Where is everyone?" Britney asked.

"It was quiet, so I sent Joan home."

Britney put her phone face down on the table as if to stop herself. "Okay, well, I have great news. You ready?"

I wasn't. I still needed to prep the beans for the morning and get the bagel order in—not to mention the other job—but she seemed adamant that whatever she had to tell me wouldn't wait. I sat across from her at the table.

"Your father wants to buy the coffee shop for you."

"So?" I asked.

"This coffee shop. He's going to buy it from me and give it to you. No loans, no nothing. Sophie talked to him, and they both want to do it."

"That's not what I want."

"They figure it's kind of like college for you. No

strings attached. It's the money they probably would have spent sending you to school and buying you a car and a condo and stuff."

I got up and returned to my duties. After the beans and bagels, I'd still need to wipe everything down and then sweep, but I'd be home within half an hour. It was always quiet in the evenings—this was definitely an early-morning crowd—but I liked to keep it open for the one or two college kids that needed to get out of their house for some peace and quiet.

"Why are you so obtuse about this?" Britney asked. She stood and all but stomped her foot in frustration. "I don't want this place anymore. You like to work here. Just accept it."

"This is not how I want to own this shop."

"I'm sorry that you were born to brilliant and successful parents, but your family has money. Why can't you just enjoy it?"

"Money doesn't bring joy," I said.

"Well, if you go too long without it, I think you'll change your mind."

I'd had this argument with Britney in various forms many times before. There seemed to be no point in responding.

"Anyway," she said, "he's working out the sales agreement with my mother. You're going to be on the deed. You may want to have a little chit-chat with them sooner, rather than later."

I called my father and asked him to talk to me.

"We can talk, sweetheart," he said. "Now is fine."

"Can you come out here to the coffee shop? Or meet me at my house?"

"Why don't you come out here? You can spend the night, if you want."

He always wanted me to spend time there at the mansion. He'd put together a library next to an office and lingered there, reading and working hour after hour. He hardly went to the company anymore, leaving Sophie and Frank to run the day-to-day operations. I figured it was because of all the memories of my mother at the company, but he wouldn't admit to that. When he goes into the office, he meets with Engineering and Fabrication on the second floor, hardly spending time on the top floor.

"No," I said. "I hate that place."

"Please don't talk like that."

"We need to talk about the coffee shop, and we should have that conversation here."

"Maybe you could come out tomorrow?" he asked.

I wanted to scream. This was the thing I noticed most since he started with Sophie, that he stonewalled me, making me do things his way. "Can we meet in Ann Arbor?"

"There's never any parking there."

This was insane: of course there was parking on a weekday evening in June. "Meet me at Mom's grave," I said.

"That's morbid."

"The sun hasn't even set. It'll be beautiful."

"I don't know."

"When was the last time you visited?"

That worked, but only partially. He drove to her section of the cemetery, but wouldn't walk to the grave.

"If you come stand by her grave," I said, "you'll feel her presence. She'll help with this decision."

"Sweetheart, it's a no-brainer. I want to buy the coffee house for you. The money is not an issue, and you'll have a thing to do from now on. For the rest of your life, if you want."

"What I want is to spend more time with you, as a family."

"Kind of hard to do that if you won't even come to the house."

"That house is the exact opposite of what Mom wanted for us."

"Sweetheart, listen—"

"You promised."

"I'm married now."

"But you won't even visit her grave."

He pushed himself up from where he'd been leaning against his car. "You're being stubborn and ridiculous."

"Just stand there at the grave and tell me about being married. I want Mom to hear it."

"That's it." He got into the car and started it.

"Dad, please."

He rolled down the window. "Think about the coffee shop. I'm not going to keep playing games. I'm not leaving my company, and I'm not leaving my wife. It's either my way or no deal."

As my father drove away, I felt the absurdity of my situation. And the shame. Everything I had in life was because of my parents. Yes, I had rejected much of what my father offered, but I had money my mother gave me before she died, and a bunch more she left for me in her will. I lived a bohemian life rejecting capitalism on principle, but I had it way easier than the young people around me who relied on paychecks.

I bought a car with that money and I could last awhile more without a job. I lived comfortably thanks to the spoils of capitalism. I was no better than a house cat hissing at the humans.

On the other hand, everyone is part of the system. You can't simply walk away and expect to get anything done. Homeless people are forced out of the system and punished for it.

I was starting to think there was no point to my protests. I should take the deal and try to live happily. Try to find a way to save my soul from how the system wanted to distort it.

A bird flew past my face, then another, and a third: starlings.

The starlings swooped around me, snatching gnats and mosquitoes and moths from the air. The sun had dipped below the trees along the edge of the cemetery and the temperature dropped. I felt a cool gust of air on my neck.

The birds looped and ducked toward the ground, changing direction and turning, circling, screeching in delight.

I walked over to my mother's grave and watched the starlings continue their acrobatics until they moved off to another part of the cemetery.

My father's soul was distorted. That was the problem. He was so caught up in the system—the game of business and making money—that he thought that was the only way to play.

Which was exactly what my mother didn't want for him. For us.

If I rejected his deal for the coffee shop, I'd have stayed out of touch with him. But I hoped to change the deal to where he at least had to meet with me. I'd have asked him to remain the owner—and deal with all the stuff that goes with it, like taxes and insurance—while I managed the coffee shop.

If he agreed to work with me, I could have kept trying to get him to quit the business that was destroying his soul.

If I walked away completely, I would have abandoned him to Sophie's influence, which was a big part of the problem.

I had to try to save him for Mom's sake, as well as mine.

# # # #

IT WAS LATE WHEN I GOT TO Mansionville. The front door was locked, and I felt weird about letting myself in after saying I hated being there. I pressed the magic doorbell button. A few moments later, my father's voice emanated from a hidden speaker.

"Ashley?" he said. "That you?"

I raised my face to the camera. "Can we talk?"

"I'm in the lounge."

The door unlocked and the atrium lights flipped on as I entered.

The lounge is a room on the lower level. I'd call it a basement, but there's nothing basement-like about it. The lower level has nine foot ceilings, a bedroom-bathroom suite, a second kitchen, and a massive, open space called the lounge. There was a bar at one end, a jukebox no one had ever used, a pool table, and couches scattered throughout.

The wall was forty feet of windows overlooking the pond. At this hour, the windows reflected the interior of the lounge, with a few spots of light from the lampposts leading down to the water poking through the images on the glass.

My dad, sprawled on the couch in front of the ginormous television watching golf, turned his head at my approach. "Hey Sweetheart."

I took a position in front of the television. I focused on my breath for several seconds. I really didn't want to have this conversation. I wanted my dad to do what was right without me telling him. This had to be what it was like for kids who caught their dad cheating and were forced to confront them. Was I wrong about this demand? If you make a promise to someone who dies, does that remove the obligation?

No. The promise was on my behalf, and I wasn't dead.

I stood in front of him, very much undead.

He turned off the television. "You okay?"

My breath was shallow, and I started to worry I

might hyperventilate, but I managed to nod my head.

"I heard Joan started today. That's pretty cool, huh?"

"Yes. Thank you for that."

"I'm sure she'll do fine."

"I want to talk about the coffee shop."

He crossed his arms and folded one leg over the other. "I told you the way it is. So do you accept my offer?"

"This is not a business negotiation," I said. "We're family. You and I are all the actual family we have."

He rolled his eyes. "Sophie loves you very much, and now you have Britney."

"Dad, I want to have you for my father. I don't want you to be the guy who married my stepmother, who says she loves me but can't really stand the sight of me."

"That's disingenuous."

I didn't want to get sucked into a debate over semantics and syntax, like we were hashing out a contract for a deal. "I'd like to do something with you, the way you and mom had the business together, and then had a family."

"You're still welcome to work with me at—"

"No. After Mom died, you weren't there for me through junior high and high school. You had the business, you had Sophie, and you had this house. You dragged me along for the ride."

He sat up and leaned forward. "A lot of kids your age would be pretty appreciative of a setup like this."

"But they wouldn't want you for their father."

He stared a hot minute at me, his eyebrows drawing closer, his eyes squeezing into a squint. "You don't want me for a father?"

I raised my arms. "That's exactly the opposite. I want you for my father. Instead, I've got this wealthy entrepreneur who thinks giving me money is the same as showering me with love."

He sat back on the couch and folded his arms again. "I can't just walk away from the company."

"Why the fuck not?" I shouted. "Give the company to the employees, like Mom said—or sell it to them. I don't care at this point—and you can hang around to consult, show them the ropes or whatever. But spend a fraction of the time you spend with the company with me. Really spend time with me, not just to go shopping or invite me on exotic cruises fueled by the labor of exploited poor people."

"Jesus fucking Christ, Ashley. That's a ton of shit you're dumping on me."

"I've been trying to spoon feed you the shit for years, but that hasn't worked."

"I don't appreciate it either way."

"Don't you see how much I love you and desperately want to be your daughter before it's too late?"

"Too late for what?"

"Too late for me to become someone who is molded by your love and guidance. Isn't that what dads are supposed to do?"

He shook his head. "You're asking the impossible of me."

"But what if something happened tomorrow that ruined your business?"

"Like what?"

"Like, I don't know, the market crashed, a competitor invents a better mousetrap, you get cancer like mom."

He laughed. He actually, fucking, laughed. "First, the market is fine, and no one is going to invent a better mousetrap than our team. I stake my career on that."

"Great."

"And I'm healthy as a horse. What happened to your mom was a tragic fluke. The odds of both of us dying of cancer are really low. Negligible, in fact."

"Oh, for fuck's sake, Dad."

"What the hell has gotten into you?"

I blathered something totally incoherent. I was so angry I wanted to slap him, or pound on his chest, yank him by the hair, something—anything—to get him to realize what he'd become. It all bounced around in my head: Mom's painful death, the horrible sadness of realizing we'd never see her again, and his infuriating joy when he started playing house with Sophie.

I paced across the room to calm down. "Does Mom ever come to you in your dreams?"

"What? Sometimes, I guess."

"Does she talk to you?"

"Not that I remember."

"Sleep on it Dad," I said. "See if she talks to you tonight. Listen to what she says. I'm begging you to do what she asks. Please?"

He picked up the remote and turned on the television. Staring at the golf match, he said, "I'll sleep on it."

8

JOAN

I brought in donuts and asked Edna where to leave them.

"You didn't have to do that," Edna said.

"I want to thank everyone for the opportunity."

"You'd best leave them with me," she said. "I'll send out a note to the team. If we put them in a common area, they'll be gone before the second pot of coffee brews."

I visited Ingrid's lab to ask what I should do, but she wasn't there. I was in my cubicle, browsing the Internet while eating a donut, when Brian stopped by.

"First, thanks for the donuts," he said. "I appreciate your selection. There was a lot of variety. Did you work in a donut shop?"

"No, a coffee shop. But we sold bagels and donuts from a local bakery. Variety is key."

"Amazing."

I didn't think he was just there about the donuts, and hoped he wasn't just checking me out. "What's up?"

"Slight change in duties. I'm going to have you work with Pat. I think he has some Windows stuff you can do."

"Sounds good."

"Great."

"I was wondering…"

Brian leaned against one of the cubicle walls, his bulk moving it a couple of inches. "Sorry, what?"

"How's your disaster recovery plan?"

"Not sure what you mean."

"I know this is dumb, but one of my professors mentioned the importance of disaster recovery plans."

"Interesting. I'm pretty sure we're all set, though."

"Right," I said. "I certainly wasn't trying to imply anything."

"We're fine," a man's voice called from the other side of the wall.

Brian smiled and hooked a thumb at the next cubicle. "You see, I knew Mike would be on this."

Mike's head appeared above the wall. He had dark hair, a thick goatee speckled gray, and his cheeks were flushed red. "We do daily backups of all the servers, which we keep for a week. We save weeklies for a month, and monthlies for a year. We have seven annual backups stored. We're fine."

"Great."

Brian gave Mike the Thumbs-up.

"What about the individual workstations and laptops?" I asked.

Mike pursed his lips. "That's Pat's problem."

"Well, there you go," Brian said. "Let's go talk to Pat."

Pat had a long face and sandy brown hair. Maybe he was blond at one point, but the hair on his head was so fine it looked like a cheap wig from a thrift shop. He was pale to a fault, like an anemic goth kid who spent too much time in the basement.

"We try to back up every device once a week," he said. "That's all the bandwidth we can stand. Each night, we back up all the servers, which takes six hours to complete. We can also back up a couple dozen desktops before seven o'clock. "

"So, once a week?" Brian asked. "That sounds safe to me."

Pat flipped a pencil and caught it. "If you want them backed up more frequently, we'll need more budget."

"I think it's fine," Brian said. He turned to me. "You agree?"

"It's all good," I said. "I wasn't casting aspersions. I just want to help."

Brian turned back to Pat. "Can she help you?"

"She can keep bringing in donuts."

"Be serious."

"Of course she can help. There must be a hundred and fifty things people have complained about. I can't get to them all."

Brian put a hand to his cheek with a dramatic flourish. "Is it that bad? I thought we had it figured out."

Pat flipped the pencil. "The last set of patches we pushed out broke some things for people. We fixed all the high priority stuff, but there's lots of other things."

Brian held out a hand as if offering me a drink from a

serving tray. "You think you can help?"

"I can try."

It turned out Edna was the keeper of problem tickets. Someone had put together a spreadsheet that Edna used to track all the calls. But I didn't have to bother her to get access.

"It's on her computer's C-drive," Pat explained, "but we just use the hidden share to update it."

"What's the hidden share?"

Pat got up and bid me to follow him with a nod of his head. He went into my cubicle and motioned for me to sit in my chair.

"Bring up a run command box," he said.

I pressed the Windows key and the R key, and the little command prompt appeared in the corner of my Windows desktop.

"Type: backslash-backslash Edna, backslash, C, dollar."

I typed:

```
\\edna\c$
```

A file explorer window appeared, listing a bunch of folders and files, presumably on Edna's desktop computer. Pat told me where to navigate to, and there was an Excel spreadsheet for all the complaints.

"This seemed simpler than putting it on one of the file servers," Pat said. "We were kind of in a hurry, hacked it together, showed Edna how to open it, and left it there. She doesn't do well with change, and it was just us, so…"

"Yeah," I said. "Makes sense."

"We have that secret share on every computer. Almost all the computers are named after the user."

"Seems simpler that way."

"Right," Pat said.

He showed me how to navigate the spreadsheet, but it was straightforward enough.

"Pick out any of those problems to work on," he said. "You'll be a hero."

I picked out a simple problem reported by Gail, secretary to Frank. She wasn't sure how to copy some file from one folder to another. I called and talked about her problem. She'd forgotten about it, recreating the files anew, because she couldn't copy them. She was redoing weeks' worth of work. It made no sense.

While we chatted, I opened a command window, typed:

```
\\gail\c$
```

A file explorer of Gail's computer drive displayed on my monitor. I found the folder of the files she wanted copied, moved them to the new folder, overwriting the files already recreated. She was so grateful.

I continued poking around Gail's computer and found a few interesting things with "frank" in the filename. No telling what people save on their computer's file system. Which gave me an idea.

Sure enough, back on Edna's computer, there was a file, an Excel Spreadsheet, called "passwords."

It was a list of passwords, alright, but passwords that Brian, Pat, Mike, Ingrid and Oscar told Edna to save. It was their technique for backing each other up on various systems.

They granted access to the various file servers via Active Directory. But there were several extra software applications installed, and web services they used, to perform various administrative bullshit. The spreadsheet of passwords allowed Oscar, for instance, to do something Pat usually did.

No one mentioned this spreadsheet to me because I wasn't on that trust level with them yet. But they forgot anyone who knew about the secret share could reach it. Or maybe they thought someone else would solve that little problem of the passwords to every server being secured only by the obscurity of the secret share.

Now that I had that list of passwords, all I had to do was decide who should live and who should die.

9

ASHLEY

I HAD NEVER INTRODUCED JOAN TO my father. Back in middle school, when he came to pick me up from her house, he waited in the car. Never met the parents or anything.

He'd probably like my version of Joan more than he likes me. Joan is brash and funny. Joan makes and takes jokes. Joan reminds me of my mother, or what I think my mother might have been at that age.

I'm curious what my mother would think about my version of Joan. Is Joan too brash, too bold, too happy? If Joan would have reminded my mother of a younger version of herself, would she be critical of Joan?

My Joan has red hair in a pixie cut. I (Ashley) have a big mop of dark hair, unkempt and without form.

Joan's ears are in plain sight and littered with studs and earrings. I hide my ears beneath that mop of dark hair.

Joan's eyes are sky blue. Well, so are mine, but I wear glasses smudged with fingerprints so you can't really see my eyes.

Joan wears tight tops, leggings or short skirts, and

high heels when possible. She'll show a lot of her smooth, tan skin.

Ashley dresses in frumpy t-shirts and loose jeans. Even in warm weather, she covers up. Heat is usually not a problem because she doesn't move around much.

Joan likes to be out on the town, visit bars, sing karaoke. She doesn't play sports, but she moves like an athlete. When Joan dances, people watch.

Ashley prefers to stay inside, reading books. In fall, she'll walk around enjoying the change of seasons and the cooler air.

For a while, Joan and Kirsten went out a lot. We got into some stuff. Joan, bankrolled by Ashley's minor fortune, could have gotten a lot worse.

It was Kirsten who blinked first. "I don't want to end up like my mom," she said. "I really want to get a degree and get a job with some potential. And I kind of miss Ashley."

"I thought you liked me as Joan," I said.

"I like Joan," she said. "But I like Ashley more. I worry Joan isn't really happy. I think Joan is acting happy, but maybe isn't."

I thought of what Kirsten said because I (Ashley) had to quit the coffee shop. Joan needed to do this thing at HD Enterprises, which meant I couldn't keep slinging coffee.

I sent Britney a text to resign. I wrote, "I quit. Sorry for the short notice."

She replied, "Seriously?"

I didn't reply.

I expected Britney to stop by my place in the evening, so I went to the cemetery to avoid her. I turned off my phone, which I always did when visiting my mother, so as not to be bothered. I needed to talk to my mom about my dad and the business. His business.

I love my dad, but does he love me?

Should I do the thing I'm thinking about doing? Should I test him like that?

It was a quiet evening. Along the road, a skinny, shirtless guy ran past, his sneakers padding gently along the road, a cap pulled low to block the sun. A few minutes later, a few cyclists pedaled by, the bike chains clicking with a gear shift, the tires churning dust on the dirt road. "Coming up," one of them said.

The grass had been cut that day and the lawn clippings were clumped together in rows, turning brown, the acrid scent of chlorophyll in the air.

I didn't bother asking my mother about what I should do. I'd explained it already and if things had gone well, I'd have been thanking her. Of course, my mother would know exactly what was going on now.

A car drove into the cemetery and made its way along the winding path. It was a Chrysler 300, my father's car. An Audi Quattro entered, which was Britney's. They parked and approached together: my father in a suit but disheveled with an unbuttoned collar, Britney dressed for tennis and clutching a water bottle.

"I'm worried about you," my father said. "I just hope

this is another stunt for attention."

"Quitting a crappy barista job is not a stunt. It's a job that shouldn't even exist."

Dad scowled. "What does that even mean?"

"I'm not improving lives by serving coffee. I'm only there to take their money and make sure the other employees don't steal."

"That's part of running a business."

"And she's not paying a living wage."

"Hey," Britney said. "I pay more than Starbucks and Biggby."

"It's still not enough."

"You're just serving coffee."

"Okay," Dad said. His face turned pink. "I'm not getting pulled into one of these anti-business things with you."

"Fine, how about we discuss how your business is more important to you than our family?"

"Britney is family, and you put her in an awkward position."

"Awkward?"

"She lost a full day's revenue because no one was there to open the shop."

I groaned. "Unlock the door, brew some coffee, and make it the honor system. People pour their own brew and pay what they want."

Dad laughed. "Now that's a stunt. Bravo."

"I'm serious. You always talk about how employees are the biggest expense. They're such a burden, so run your little coffee shop business without them."

Dad walked back to his car.

Britney raised a hand. "To be clear, are you going to open the coffee shop in the morning?"

"No."

"You're done?"

"Yes."

"I told you," Dad said. "That's what she's like." He drove off.

Britney sipped her water. "Thanks."

My stomach twisted. It hit me that I might also have alienated Britney. In horror, I worried that quitting without thinking about what she needed or how she'd feel about it was as bad as what Dad did to me. It felt like my brain was short circuiting and my face was on fire.

"It's nothing personal," I said. I stepped closer, thinking I might hug her, or maybe throw myself at her feet. She didn't seem receptive to any contact, so I stopped. "I really like you. You've been a good stepsister."

She raised the water bottle to me, offered a half-smile, and walked back to her car.

Stepsister is not enough. It wasn't her fault Sophie married my dad. I hurried to her car. "You're a wonderful sister."

She opened her car door but paused there. "You should have called me first. Okay?"

"I'm really sorry. Are you mad?"

"Yes, but we'll be okay."

"I didn't mean to hurt you."

She hugged me. It was such a relief, and I almost burst into tears as the mix of emotions bubbled up. I couldn't remember the last time my dad hugged me. My legs shook, and I had to swallow a few times before I calmed down.

"You going?" she asked.

"I need to talk to my mom."

Britney glanced around—we were the only ones left. "Don't hang around too much longer."

She left, and the cemetery grew quiet. The starlings winged past in the darkness. A warm, comfortable sensation spread over me. I wasn't worried about anything, and I remembered one of the last times my mom hugged me like a mom, pulling me close and holding me, rubbing my back. It was just before she went into the hospital for the last time.

"What should I do?" I asked.

I heard my mother say, "Do it."

10

JOAN

ANY IDIOT CAN SET FIRE TO the building. You don't even need a reason.

To pull it off and get away with it is still amateur hour. Find the blind spots in the security cameras. Cut the phone lines so the alarms can't summon help. Start the accelerant in a place that won't be seen from the road. Leave nothing behind.

Just like it says on the internet.

But to have leverage, to twist their arm behind their back and make them say, "Uncle," and get what you want—what you deserve—takes skill.

As the Wicked Witch of the West said, "These things must be done delicately."

The first principle was to understand all the processes and how the IT department would react. Would they come together as one and fix the problems? Would they struggle and fracture, blaming each other? Did they even have a plan to recover?

They didn't have a plan. The admins were convinced their redundant server backups covered their ass. In truth, their ass cheeks flapped in the wind.

Although they could have used those backups to recover to a point in time, I knew it would take days to accomplish. Their business systems had interdependencies. Those servers worked together. Nothing would be restored until everything was restored.

The servers were useless without the employee computers to access them. They had three hundred employees, and each one had a computer. They left those computers on every night for the backups to run, which exposed them to attack.

Once the malware encrypted those four hundred machines, the IT department would be overwhelmed. Business operations wouldn't operate.

I also knew that I'd be blamed. I was the outsider. The new person. The friend of the boss's daughter.

They'd turn on me quickly, but the evidence would lead elsewhere. In that short time on the job, I discovered that Jared, a junior executive, had an internet browser history of gambling and pornography websites. How did I discover that?

The secret-but-not-secure share of every computer on the network allowed me to look at the history cached on Jared's laptop. I snooped at a few other candidates— two of the engineers, for instance, indulge gambling habits at work—but it was almost too easy with Jared. There was already a malware script downloaded to his laptop, but he hadn't clicked on it. He had recent activity on OnlyFans.com and AshleyMadison.com, among others.

Were I to guess, it was because of his friendship with

Oscar, the firewall guy. Maybe they played online poker together, or went to strip clubs, but Jared's computer had been granted wider access to the internet.

I found half-a-dozen other employees with a sketchy browsing history in less than ten minutes of snooping. Some people were running eBay businesses, others visited 4chan and 8chan and other conspiracy-theory, nut-job sites.

Jared seemed a great option for the amount of effort I put into the search.

"What about the employees?" I wondered. This was a week before, when I visualized how it could happen.

I had to think like Ashley to consider the consequences. "This was your idea."

"This was *our* idea. I liked it because I don't care about the employees. You, however, do."

"We can't make it permanent."

"It will be chaos," I said. "I can't predict what will happen once the attack occurs."

"What do you think will happen?"

There was a case study in the 100-level class for cyber-security. In it, a trusted team of people worked on identifying the source of the infection. They brought in a specialist, and the police.

I knew HD Enterprises would react similarly. Their first step would be to understand the problem. No one outside that team would be trusted. I (Joan) would be the prime suspect.

Ashley wondered if we could program the

ransomware to expire after a day?

Of course we could have, but would that give Ashley enough time to talk to Dad? He would likely be in crisis mode until it's resolved.

Ashley didn't want to destroy anyone: not Dad, and not the employees who had done nothing wrong. But I knew he'd have to be pushed to the edge of destruction to make him consider what matters in life.

There's no way to avoid hurting people with a thing like this.

For the record, I didn't learn how to launch a ransomware attack at community college. The class talked about the situations and how to react. Not how to attack.

Luckily, there are marketplaces on the Internet that sell you kits to build a script that launches a ransomware attack.

With a little research, I learned how to be anonymous on the Internet so that, once you found what you needed, you could buy it, and download it, and nobody would know what you did.

It's simple: start with a logless VPN; use that to set up a ghost machine running Tails; use a Tor-based browser to hide all traces of your activity. That makes you anonymous.

Second, I bought cryptocurrency with cash from an ATM, used a paper wallet to get things uploaded, and used a fresh, anonymous crypto wallet that generated new Bitcoin addresses as needed.

I used the cryptocurrency to buy the ransomware kits and spent a few hours learning how to build an attack. I used the list of known machines to speed up the infection sequence, and a snippet of code to cannibalize that script so that no one would see how it happened.

It was easy to ensnare all the computers in the building.

Finally, I put everything on a thumb drive. Oh, and I bought the thumb drive with cash from the student bookstore in Ann Arbor, where I would blend in with the crowd. I carried the thumb drive into the office in my bra.

Then I wiped my laptop clean to remove all traces of my activity because I wasn't going to make a habit of this.

I figured the IT guys would work like dogs to fix it, but they would probably give up and attempt to recover from backups. Restoring those 400 computers might take a week. They could recover, but they'd lose business and innocent people will lose money from their paychecks.

As Ashley, I wasn't so sure about it.

As Joan, I knew that the bosses, including Dad, would care about the money.

Ashley hesitated, but Joan knew threatening the money was the only way to get his attention.

Money insulates the rich from trouble. A barista gets hours cut and they can't make rent. Cut the hours of a barista, who is also a single mom and maybe their kid doesn't get dinner tonight.

To attack the rich, you attack their money. Yeah, some of the working folks may not make rent, and a bunch of kids may go hungry, but that's necessary to make Dad think.

Sophie and Frank and that asshole Jared would sweat and get upset, but I didn't think they'd feel threatened. I figured the attack might cut into their travel plans, like they might have only spent ten days in Florence. But I hoped it would make them think.

Ashley was worried about the collateral damage.

I'm someone who doesn't give two shits about a lot of things.

Ashley cares about everybody.

It was like one of those internal dialog things where you think about stealing candy, or parking in a no-parking zone, or peeing behind a building. Do you want the candy? Are you in a hurry? Do you really, *really* have to pee?

I hoped that made us a good team. Ying and yang. Heckle and Jeckle. Abbott and Costello, whoever they are.

Dr. Frankenstein and his monster.

We compromised. Before executing the plan, I loaded up images of a few key laptops: Dad's, Sophie's, Frank's, the head engineer, and all their secretaries. All of it went on a two-terabyte drive bought at Staples. This delayed the plan because I couldn't move all that data during the day or Mike, the network admin, would have coughed up a hairball finding whatever was slowing down his precious network.

Also, I put in a decrypt option: enter a password and you get out of jail.

I lit the fuse on Friday afternoon, when people were leaving early for the weekend. Half the IT team was gone, the parking lot was almost empty, and I knew for sure that Jared was gone for the day. I saw him walk out with his briefcase, a duffel bag, and a shit-eating grin.

First, I took the thumb drive out of my bra, stuck it in the extra laptop stashed in my desk, and copied the script to Jared's laptop.

Next, I spoofed his MAC address on the spare laptop and browsed a known malware-infected website. That put an entry in the firewall logs to point the investigation at Jared.

Last, I used the Terminal Services utility to remotely launch the script from his laptop.

I didn't stick around to see what happened, but I had a pretty good idea how it went down. At five-thirty, the script insulated itself on Jared's laptop, turning off the anti-virus software, infecting the hard drive's master boot record, and attacking other machines.

The company's main security flaw was that they used a castle defense. There was only one way onto their network—through the firewall—and they trusted all machines inside the building. They didn't imagine anyone purposely infecting the machines from the inside.

The script exploited the hidden shares on each computer, running in the background, quietly infecting all 400 of them within fifteen minutes. At six o'clock, the encryption sequence began. If anyone was still working and noticed their computer running slowly, they'd probably took that as a sign to call it a day.

Most troubling, I hoped, would be that the systems

simply wouldn't work. Malware usually taunts the victims and demands ransom. This script wouldn't negotiate, simply prompting for the "magic word." If they guessed the magic word, the script would undo the damage.

Okay, so I suppose the script taunted them a little. My intention was to offer a puzzle wrapped in an enigma. No clues, so no sign of who might have done it.

They would blame me, the new person, despite the evidence pointing to Jared's laptop. He would deny everything. Guys like that never admit fault or take the blame. Everyone knows he's that type of guy and would nod along with his protests, but would agree behind his back he must have done something.

No one would understand why this quixotic script would simply grind their systems to a halt.

Eventually, Dad would see that his little baby, this multi-million dollar business, was as fragile as Mom's health.

Joan would vanish and, hopefully, Ashley could convince Dad that there were more important things in life.

11

BRITNEY

Britney let herself into the house and went directly to the kitchen, expecting to find Marta preparing a meal. Sophie often hosted on Friday evenings, but the kitchen was quiet. No sign of Marta.

She was there to recruit help with Ashley, who had been avoiding her all week—to the point of not showing up at work. It was almost certainly Ashley's way of avoiding the proposition to take over the coffee shop. Why she thought Ashley, who had moved out of the house to avoid her parents, would now be ready to grapple with owning a business was all about projecting. She wanted it to happen and so she wanted Ashley to be ready. Clearly, she needed help to close this deal.

Britney peered out the back, thinking that perhaps Sophie was taking a tennis lesson. Again, no signs of life.

There was a bustling from the direction of David's office. All the better, as she really wanted to talk to David.

"Hey Dad," she said, leaning into his home office doorway. "Got a second?"

"I don't got a second," he said. David slammed his laptop shut and stared at it, slowly shaking his head. "I got a virus."

"You or the computer?"

"The computer."

"Ashley fixed mine, you know."

David shook his head. "All the computers. All of them. Every fucking one is locked up."

"Oh. Shit."

"Yeah."

"Have you seen Ashley, though?"

David tossed his laptop into his valise and closed the latch. "She can't help with this," he said. "This is a big problem."

Britney sensed his energy starting to move away. "Actually, I just want to know if you've seen her. She hasn't been showing up at the coffee shop—"

"That's your problem. Your shop, your employee. I can't get involved."

"But she's your daughter. Don't you even—"

"Okay, I'll call her from the car," David said. He slipped on his suit coat and grabbed the valise as he walked out from behind the desk. "I'll tell her to call you. I wouldn't pay her, by the way."

Britney followed him down the hall toward the front door. "It's not about the money."

"I'm sure she's fine."

"Don't you want to know what's up with her?"

David trotted down the front steps toward his car.

"She's moody," he called back. "Her mother was like that sometimes."

Britney pulled the door shut. Good lord, what was going on? She'd tried to call Ashley as she drove here, not wanting to drive all the way out to Ypsi, but the phone had gone straight to voicemail, which was, naturally, full.

She found an open bottle of chardonnay in the fridge and poured a tall one. She needed energy to figure out next-steps. Thinking of next-steps reminded her that her feet hurt, and she slipped off her shoes.

Really, the coffee shop was fine. At least the girls were showing up and hadn't burned the place down (although that wouldn't be a tragedy, either). Still, she wanted to be done with it.

She topped off her wine glass and headed upstairs.

Sophie was on the couch, staring at her phone. Her glasses were at the end of her nose and she only glanced up a second at Britney.

"You okay?" Britney asked.

"In fact, no. I'm expecting a call and it's not a good time, so…"

"Could you get David to check on Ashley, or maybe send someone to check on Ashley?"

"Why would I do that?"

"Because he seems to be ignoring his daughter."

Sophie leaned back and crossed one leg over the other, flipping her shoe on and off the heel with her toes. "Have you met Ashley? I think she likes to be ignored. It's her love language, or some such bullshit. Besides, why don't you go?"

"She's actively avoiding me."

"Now you know how I feel."

Before Britney could say anything else, Sophie held up her hand to stop Britney and hit a button on the phone with her other hand. She turned her head to look past Britney as she waited for an answer.

A cooking show was on the television but without the sound. Sophie hadn't cooked anything in her life as far as Britney knew. She hardly ate the food cooked by the various housekeepers they'd gone through over the years, subsisting on wine and envy.

Sophie slammed the phone down on the coffee table. "Fucking idiot."

"Anyone I know?"

"Frank, if you must. We're supposed to meet each Friday to discuss the office, of course, but he's incommunicado at the moment."

"Have you asked David to check on him?"

Sophie leaned forward and studied her. "What's that supposed to mean?"

"I'm not sure," Britney said. "I just think someone, not me, should go check on Ashley."

The phone rang and Sophie motioned for Britney to leave. "I have to take this."

Britney stepped out and pulled the door but lingered there in the hallway. She felt like a twelve-year-old spying like that, but couldn't pull herself away.

"Where the hell are you?" Sophie asked.

As Britney sipped her wine and listened to the one-sided conversation, she couldn't help but think it was the voice of a hurt lover scolding her beau. That didn't seem possible, as she'd seen nothing of the sort before. But, then, she hadn't been around Sophie that much lately, what with tennis and law school and then the coffee shop. Her mother had taken lovers in the past, so...

"Who's that I hear?" Then, "That was most certainly not the television." Then, "What sort of game are you playing, Francis?"

The last was delivered in a tone Britney knew all too well: Sophie was about to go ballistic. Britney hurried down the hall as quickly and quietly as possible.

12

ASHLEY

ON SATURDAY MORNING, I DRANK TEA on the back steps and watched the birds and squirrels. I'd kept a dozen feeders and checked them every evening, including days when it rained. It bothered me to think that any of my neighbors would go hungry when seeds were so cheap.

The yard was a mess, but I didn't care. It was an old house with overgrown flower beds. The detached garage needed paint. I took care of the vegetable garden beside it, but that was the only bright spot.

Trees along the edge of the yard left most of the back lawn in shade, and I'd allowed whatever took root to remain, thinking it would benefit the insects. Of course, strange collections of plants grew from the spilled seeds.

The natural chaos out back is what I preferred to anything. I would spend most Saturdays at the coffee shop, but here I was free to do what I wanted. There were several books stacked beside the sofa inside, and that was my only plan for the day: feed the birds, feed the squirrels, and read books. Maybe a nap.

A loud pounding on the front door startled me. From the backyard, I heard Britney calling my name.

I walked around the house. "What's up?"

Britney was typing on her phone and glared at me for a second before finishing the message on her phone. "Where were you?"

"Out back."

"Talking to the birds or whatever?"

"Sort of."

"Dad's company was hit with a virus or something. Sophie asked me to ask you where Joan is."

"I haven't seen her."

"Can you call her?"

"Sure, but don't they have her number at work?"

Britney raised her hands. "I don't fucking know. I'm guessing she's not answering, and they're hoping she'll talk to you."

I went in the front door and made a show of tracking down my phone, which was powered off.

"That explains why you weren't answering my calls," Britney said. "I guess I should have a bird send you a message."

"Sorry, but I was just relaxing."

"Must be nice. You know, if you wanted a week off from work you just had to ask."

I didn't want to get into it with her, so I waited for my phone to start. Notifications popped up about the calls and messages, mostly from my dad, and a few from numbers not in my contacts.

I dialed Joan's phone number and put it on speaker so Britney could listen. It went to a generic voice mail message from the Verizon voice. "Call me as soon as you can." I followed up with a text message.

"She didn't text you or anything?"

I showed Britney the phone.

"Fuck."

"What did Joan do?"

"Plenty. My mother all but screamed at me to track down Joan. I heard Jared and Frank shouting at each other in the background."

"How's Dad?"

Britney busily typed a message on her phone. "I have no idea. Sophie's call woke me up, so that's my starting point."

"Maybe I should go talk to Dad."

"Where does Joan live? I've got to track her down."

"I'm not exactly sure."

"She's your best friend."

"I never went there. Joan always came here, or we hung out at the coffee shop. She's kind of nomadic."

"Where did we send her paychecks?"

"We gave her cash, remember? You didn't want to deal with the paperwork."

Britney covered her face. "Fuckity-fuck-fuck me."

"They don't have her address at dad's company?"

"Jared signed her up as a contractor, not an employee. She's just Joan LLC to them, and the money goes directly to a bank. But she hasn't even been there long enough to get paid."

"Oh."

"Yeah."

"At least she's consistently vague."

Britney grabbed one of the books from the pile on the coffee table and flipped through its pages, as if the answer might lie within.

"Do you think she did something?"

"I really don't care." Britney's phone rang, and she silenced it. "I just want Sophie to calm the fuck down and leave me alone."

She moved to the door and waved.

"You're going?"

"I own a coffee shop, remember? I thought maybe I'd stop in. Care to come down and help me?"

I shook my head.

"Didn't think so."

# # # #

AFTER BRITNEY LEFT, MY HEART STARTED POUNDING and my stomach tightened. I hadn't thought about how it would feel to sabotage a multi-million dollar business, especially one owned by my father, and I didn't want him to be mad at me. I know I'd done it because I was mad at him, but now I kind of wished I hadn't.

When Kirsten and I used to go shoplifting, I did it as Joan. But later on, as Ashley, I suffered these pangs of guilt that twisted my guts and made my skin itch.

That's how I felt.

I called my father's cell phone but Cassie, his

secretary, answered. "What is it Ashley? Your father's really busy."

"I want to talk to him."

"I'll let him know you called."

"Thanks."

I texted him, "Dad, please call me."

The reply on his phone said: "This is Cassie. He'll talk to you later."

So, technically, he didn't reply.

I knew Joan would cause trouble for them, but I didn't think it'd happen this quickly. At least it was supposed to be found out on Monday, and I was going to use this weekend to connect with my dad. I wanted to remind him, over and over, that I wanted us to have a life together, not a business.

Anyway, I didn't really know what else to do—ordinarily, I'd be working at the coffee shop—so I went down to HD Enterprises.

There were two dozen cars in the lot. The front door was locked, but the security guard let me in.

"I'm Ashley Rice," I said. "David Rice's daughter." I had the wig on, the thick-framed glasses, and my frumpy clothes. I folded my arms across my chest and I stared at the floor.

He was the guy I'd first met as Joan, but nothing about his posture or looks suggested he recognized me. He let me in but asked me to wait in the lobby. "Everybody is pretty uptight right now. I'll call, but I'm not sure they want to talk to you unless you can solve the problem."

"What's the problem?"

"Security issue."

"I hope everything's okay."

"It will be," he said, but the look on his face said otherwise.

After about fifteen minutes, Cassie came down. She wore glasses and tucked her blond hair under a ball cap. She was in jeans, sneakers, and a T-shirt, and wore a blazer over the shirt. "Your father won't be able to see you for a while."

"You can't be serious."

"It's serious."

I wanted to scream, or cry, or maybe both, but I settled on sitting back on the sofa and staring at my shoes.

"Are you okay?" Cassie asked. "You look pale."

"You're wearing too much makeup," I said.

Cassie blinked. "Excuse me?"

"I need to go home."

"I'll tell him you stopped by."

I returned to my house and paced. I needed to talk to my dad, but didn't know how long it'd be until he made himself available. Obviously, this was not part of the plan.

I texted him, "I have something you'll want to see."

He called. "What is it?"

"It's a thing from Joan."

"But what is it?"

"I'm not sure, but I think it's a hard drive."

"External storage?"

"I guess."

"I'm sending someone over."

"No! I need to—"

He hung up before I could insist he talk to me.

Ten minutes later, Cassie and Jared knocked on my door. This was the first time Jared had ever met Ashley. I stood in the door, waiting.

Cassie waved. "You told your father you have something, a hard drive?" If I hurt her feelings with the makeup comment earlier, she did a great job covering up the pain.

I closed the door and retreated to my couch, where I pulled a blanket over my head. My heart pounded, and I wanted to puke. I needed to be Joan to get through this, but I couldn't let them see Joan.

They talked outside the door, but I couldn't understand what they said. They knocked, then they pounded.

"Ashley?" Jared called.

The door opened, and they walked in.

"Ashley?" Cassie said. "Are you here? Do you want us to wait?"

"We're waiting," Jared said.

"I don't think she wants to talk to us."

"Too bad for Ashley." Jared walked across the room.

"Wait," Cassie said. "I think she's on the couch."

"Here?"

"Yes."

"Ashley?" Jared asked. "Are you on the couch?"

"Yes."

"Will you give us the hard drive, please?"

"No."

"Is it because you want to talk to your dad?"

"I want to see my dad."

Jared walked again, and I heard them whisper.

"Is there an actual hard drive?" Jared asked.

"I want to see my dad."

"We'll take you to him," Cassie said.

"But you have to give us the hard drive," Jared added.

"Tell him to come here."

They were silent for a while. Jared said, "You're not going to pull that blanket off of your head?"

I shook my head. I didn't know if they could see that, but I didn't care.

"Let's go," Cassie said.

"What a fucking mess," Jared said.

Half an hour later, my dad walked in the front door. His hair was mussed, like he'd been roused from bed, threw on some casual-yet-wealthy-looking clothes, and raced down to headquarters.

I was still on the sofa but had pulled the blanket aside. I was wearing what I slept in.

"What is going on, Ashley?" he asked. "This is not a time when I can just wander away from my office to see you. I mean, I love you and all, but this is not a good time for shenanigans."

"Sorry. So very sorry for the shenanigans."

"Not funny, okay? Do you have any idea what's happening to us?"

"The security guy said there was an issue."

"Yeah. An issue. Like an existential crisis that could cost us millions of dollars. Millions."

"Sorry for your loss," I said.

He closed the door and scanned the room, as if someone might be eavesdropping. "Brian, the I.T. manager, thinks your little friend, Joan, has something to do with our issue. That Joan, whom I recommended for a job based on your request, may have caused irreparable damage. She's been there a week and she cost us millions of dollars."

"Money isn't everything."

He nodded, his lips pressed together tightly like he was chomping his own flesh in spite. "I know where you're going with this, but I don't have time. I know we haven't been as close as any of us hoped after your mother died. I miss her too, you know. But this is not the time to have that discussion. So whatever it is, especially if it has to do with Joan, I need to know it and have it right now. No more kidding around."

My nausea passed, but blood rush to my face. I was angry, again, at my dad. "What if your company goes out of business today?"

"Why would you ask such a thing?"

"I want to know what you would do? Would you talk to me then? Would you spend time with me and be more like a father?"

He cleared some space on my coffee table and sat down. It was the closest to me he'd been in months. "My company is beset by a terrible disaster, and you're trying to make it about you."

"What? No."

"Of course you are," he said. "It's not fair."

"Goddamit, Dad." I jumped up from the couch and got the hard drive, which I'd stashed at the bottom of the trash can under the plastic bag. "Joan said something about you needing this."

"She did this then?"

"No."

He glanced at the hard drive and shook his head.

"She told me that Jared was looking at porn sites. She saw a virus or something on his computer, so she took an extra backup, just in case. That's probably where it started."

He walked to the door and shook his head again. "Why the hell would she have whatever is on here? Why would she have this backup?"

"I just said because she was worried."

"Sounds fishy."

"Jared is visiting sketchy websites, and she took some personal initiative to save data before disaster happened, but I guess that sounds fishy."

"Quite the coincidence."

"There are amazing coincidences every single day, but we don't notice them because we think everything is fine. We think we're going to be okay. Then something bad happens and finally we notice one of the amazing coincidences, if only to blame the innocent and uninvolved."

"Okay, now you're being ridiculous."

"Maybe they aren't coincidences, but are part of a cosmic plan to bring us together, and remind us how our love for each other is all that matters."

He nodded. "You're thinking about your mother again."

"I'm always thinking about her. To me, everything is about her."

He put his hand on the door but paused. "Tell Joan to talk to us. I'd like to help her."

"She doesn't need any help."

"She better get a lawyer. Once we prove she did this, charges will be pressed. Lawsuits will be filed. I wouldn't want to be her with all this trouble brewing."

"Do you know any lawyers who specialize in shenanigans?"

13

JOAN

THAT ASSHOLE JARED SENT ABOUT A dozen emails and text messages telling me I had to show up, confess, and otherwise commit ceremonial disembowelment on the steps of the company or they were going to drop a bomb on my head. Frank sent a few himself, and then another from Brian, each one riffing on this theme that I had betrayed them and caused great damage and havoc, etc., to their beloved and holy business of making money from toxic industrial sites and they couldn't save any more babies because I was a bad person. It seemed like they were inviting me to my beheading.

I didn't want to show up empty-handed, but what does one bring to a beheading?

Donuts.

I brought three dozen boxed donuts, a mix of crullers and glazed and sugar-coated and cream-filled and jelly-filled and custard-filled. Bear claws and Long John and éclairs and twists and cake with icing and cake with sprinkles and plain.

Plain donuts are the forgotten stepchild of the donut industry, but I brought two of them that day.

I gave the first box to Vince at the security desk and asked him to do with them whatever he thought was best.

He peeked inside the box. "Did you get a Bavarian cream?"

I offered the box and pointed at the donut he wanted.

"I"ll just take that one, thanks."

"You mad at me?"

He bit into the donut and breathed deeply while the sugar hit his throat. "I don't know any specifics. If I lose my job, I might be mad."

"If you lose your job, I'll be mad too."

I noticed Vince glancing at me. I'd worn a red, scoop-neck T-shirt. Yes, there was cleavage. My jeans were form-fitting and comfortable. The shoes, I admit, were for show: black platform mules. I had painted my toenails bright red.

"So you came straight from church?"

I laughed.

Across the lobby, the elevator opened, and Brian approached. "You think this is a party?"

"I was thinking more like brunch," I said.

"Brunch would have eggs and sliced melon," Vince said.

Brian glared at him. "So it's a joke?"

"It's donuts," Vince said. "Relax."

"Frank and Sophie are not interested in donuts," Brian said. "This is a serious matter."

I carried the donuts to Vince's desk. "Can you find a

home for these?"

"Throw them away," Brian said.

I let him have the last word. When guys in their thirties have tasted management, they can't wait for their chance to act like a boss. They bark out orders until a bigger dog shows up. They want everyone to know they've made a decision, or settled the matter. In the coffee shop, it plays out like a tantrum, a big baby stomping its feet until it gets what it wants, even if it's more caramel sauce on the whipped cream topping their macchiato.

But ensconced in the elevator, away from a subordinate other than myself, I had another idea. "If he throws those donuts away," I said, "you'll go dumpster diving to find one. I got your favorite, and I know you could smell it."

"You won't be so clever when the police take you away in handcuffs."

Okay. I let him have *that* last line.

# # # #

MY I.T. TEAMMATES CROWDED INTO ONE END of the conference room on the second floor. Laptops covered half the table, with cables and power adapters piled and twisted together in the middle.

The other end of the conference table, where Frank, Jared, and Brian sat, was tidy. Brian had a pad of paper covered with notes. Frank and Jared rested their elbows on the table, their faces somber as they stared at me.

"What do you want?" Frank asked.

"Huh?"

"This stunt you pulled. What do you want to end it?"

There were seven men at the table and each one stared at little old me. "Nice to see that the patriarchy is still intact," I said.

Jared scoffed. "Don't start that shit."

"Sorry. But you have to admit it's like cosplay for Snow White and the Seven Little People?"

Frank slapped the table. "None of us are in the mood."

"No one has told me what's going on so maybe we should start there."

Jared scoffed. "Cut the crap. You know what this's about."

Frank waved his hand at Jared. Pointing at Brian, he said, "Fine. Tell her what you told us."

Brian flipped back a couple of pages on his notepad. "A malicious script has attacked all our servers, laptops and personal computers on site using various exploits to infect with malware."

"Ransomware," Mike said.

"I was getting to that," Brain said. "Starting around six o'clock Friday evening, the script encrypted each device, rendering them useless. When the operating system starts, the script displays a blank screen and prompts for a 'Magic Word.' We think that by entering the magic word, the device will decrypt and return to normal operation. There is no request for ransom—not that we'd pay it—but we believe you may have something to do with it."

Neither Brian nor any of my teammates made eye contact. "So, what are you asking me?"

"What's the magic word?" Brian said.

"Excuse me?"

Jared slapped his hand on the table, like his Uncle Frank had done a minute before. "What's the magic word?"

"Are you serious?"

"Yes, goddammit."

Frank waved his hand at Jared again. "Yes, we're serious. What's the magic word?"

"Please."

Frank sighed and shook his head. "Fine. What's the magic word, please?"

"I meant, have you tried using the word 'please?'"

"Oh, for fuck's sake," Jared said. "I told you this would be a waste of time."

"Wait," Brian said. "Have we tried 'please?'"

Mike, Pat and Oscar exchanged looks.

"Seriously?" Brian said. "No one tried the word 'please?'"

"Okay," Mike said. "I'll try." He pulled a laptop within reach and typed on the keyboard. He shook his head.

I rapped my hands on the table—if they could slap, I could rap—to get Oscar's attention. "Have you tried setting up a script for a brute force check of passwords? Is that what you want me to do?"

"No," Brian said. "You're not here to tell us what to do. We're not listening to your advice. And you're not touching any of our equipment ever again."

I scoffed, trying my best to sound like Jared. "You think I did this?"

"Yes," Jared said. "You absolutely did this, and I can't wait until you're in jail, and then we sue you into poverty for the rest of your life."

Frank leaned over and whispered to Jared, who shook his head as he got up and headed for the door.

"There are donuts downstairs," I said.

Frank smiled at me. "We don't want this to be contentious. You've endangered this company and the livelihoods of over three hundred people. Tell us the password and that will be the end. I promise."

That promise and a dollar bill wouldn't even get me a cup of coffee at McDonalds. Jared's threats worried me a bit because he seemed the type to get violent, showing off his manhood and all. "I'd love to help you, but I know nothing about how this happened. And I'm insulted that you think I do."

Brian scoffed. It was the most aggressive thing I'd heard him do in the short time I'd known him. "You took an odd interest in our network architecture and asked specifically about disaster recovery."

"So I'm interested. It's what I studied in school."

"You seem a bit like a fireman setting fires to come in and save the day."

"I haven't saved the day, though."

"You know what I mean."

Frank cleared his throat. "It seems odd that you had backups of the executive team's laptops."

"What's odd," I said, "is that your disaster recovery plan depended on recovering from backups, yet you didn't backup individual computers more than once a week. I took those backups as a favor to my friend, Ashley, whose father was kind enough to bring me here. I saw an egregious and risky attitude for the well-being of this company and I took one tiny action to protect what I could, using my money to buy that backup device."

Frank nodded, drummed his fingers on the table. "Anything else you want to tell us?"

I drummed my fingers on the table, copying Frank's rhythm. "There's no off-site or cold storage of backups, leaving you vulnerable to fire or anything, really. You have an unprotected share on every computer in the building. And you didn't block Jared at the firewall from viewing porn or gambling sites. And he wasn't the only one. Did you guys ever do a penetration test?"

Frank looked at Brian, who in turn looked at Mike. Mike shook his head.

"So what happened," I said, "seemed like it was bound to happen. I'm not an arsonist. I'm not a hacker from the dark web. I'm just a second-year student at a community college but I knew enough to know that you guys had a terrible system in place."

Brian's lips trembled, and his nostrils flared. "The only problem with our system is that we didn't expect someone we trusted to stab us all in the back."

"I'm willing to help solve this problem," I said. "But I don't think any of you want that."

"You've done enough," Brian said.

"I assume I'll be paid for this hour?"

Brian scoffed.

"Then I'll see you later."

14

Frank followed me across the floor to the elevators. As I waited, he stood over me, his breath reeking of coffee. "I want that password."

I sent a text to Vince, the security guy, asking him to come get me, and backed up into the cubicle area. This was a bit more than dealing with an idiot at the coffee shop. "I'm sure you do, but I don't know it."

He smiled, but it wasn't because of an effervescent joy building in his soul. It was a sad attempt to put me at ease. It was uncharacteristic for me as Joan, but my legs trembled. I rested a hand on a chair to steady myself. I slipped my other hand into my back pocket, where I had a small can of pepper spray.

"We don't have to be adversaries," Frank said. "You've done this thing, and maybe you're bad at it and forgot to include the ransom note, or maybe you're an anarchist who wants to mess things up. Maybe trying to stick it to the man?"

"None of the above," I said.

"Think about it," he said. "Decide who you want to

be: my friend who has shown some skills with business disruption, or my enemy who doesn't know what real trouble is."

He jotted down something on the back of a business card. "That's my personal cell phone. Only a couple of people have that number, okay? I'll answer at any time of day."

I slipped the card in my pocket with the pepper spray. "I won't call."

"You should. The sooner the better."

The elevator arrived and Vince leaned out. "Going down?"

I stepped inside.

Frank flipped me off as the doors closed.

# # # #

WHEN I PAID THIS VISIT, I CHOSE not to drive my car because the visits to Ashley's house had been intense. I worried that someone would run the plates on the car, realize it was Ashley's and I'd lose what little leverage we had.

I had arranged an Uber to come get me—same way I got there—but it'd be a few minutes because the closest one was at the airport. I should have planned that better, but I hadn't known what to expect when I arrived.

"Do you know what you're doing?" Vince asked.

"As much as anyone knows."

The elevator doors opened and Jared was waiting, flanked by two uniformed sheriff's deputies. Brown shirts, big guts, hair on the upper lip.

"I hope you don't mind," Vince said, "but I offered them donuts."

"Piggies gotta' eat," I whispered.

"Joan," Jared called to me. "The local constable would like a word."

One deputy took out a notepad and pen while the other stepped in my path. "Ma'am, we have a few questions. They've offered the use of a conference room, if that would be alright with you."

I walked around him and helped myself to a donut —a Bismarck, dusted in sugar and a red jelly stain on its side.

"Ma'am," the deputy said. "I'm Detective Smith. Serious allegations have been made."

"I'm Detective Brown," the other deputy said. "You may be in serious trouble. It's in your best interest to talk with us now, before things escalate."

I winked at Vince and walked out the door. I went to the curb and turned so that the sun would be at my back.

Smith positioned himself in front of me. "If you'd prefer, we can go to the station, have a friendly talk about these allegations."

"We can get you some coffee," Brown said. "Wash down that jelly donut."

For no particular reason, I shoved the better part of that donut in my mouth and chewed, breathing through my nose.

"We're trying hard to be polite," Smith said. "But if half of what Mr. Marshall says is true, you're in some serious legal trouble."

My ride arrived. I raised my hand, holding the last part of the donut to signal him.

"We could arrest you," Brown said. "You maybe think we won't, but we just might."

The car pulled up to the curb, and I walked around the detectives, avoiding eye contact like I was in a bar and making my way to the Ladies restroom. I think what prevented them from detaining me is that they didn't understand what was going on.

If they knew how hard and fast my heart was beating, they would have dragged my ass down to the station.

15

SOPHIE

Sophie carried three donuts in her hands, each wrapped in a napkin, and offered one to Gail.

"I shouldn't," she said. "They're so many calories."

"I'm here to tell you it's okay."

"Thank you."

Sophie nodded toward the closed door of Frank's office. "Would you mind?"

"I think he's on the phone."

"Just open the door, dear," Sophie said.

"I can let him know you want to see him."

Sophie breathed in and raised her head, looking down her nose at Gail. "Open that fucking door this second."

Gail's chair tipped over as she got up and opened the office door, allowing Sophie to pass through, and closed the door. Sophie thought Gail had actually done everything just right.

Frank was on his phone, standing at the window. He glanced over his shoulder at Sophie. "I'll call you back."

"Something important?" Sophie asked.

"No."

Sophie took a bite of the donut as she placed the other on Frank's desk. "Who was it?"

"A friend."

"Anyone I know?"

Frank shook his head and took up the donut. She'd given him the plain, which she knew he disliked. He took a bite and smiled.

"Thanks," he said, and took a second bite.

Sophie tossed her donut, a chocolate cake with chocolate frosting, into the trash can. "You've been distant lately. Have you been avoiding me?"

Frank took another bite of the donut and shook his head.

"Shall we meet up north tonight?"

Frank wiped his mouth. "I'm guessing I'll be swamped with all of this."

"Such a waste," Sophie said, "to have a cottage on Torch Lake and not use it in beautiful weather. What's the point?"

"I'll see if I can get away."

"And then there's the matter of me."

"You know I care for you."

"But I'm like that cottage, going to waste, gathering dust."

"It's just been a busy time."

She opened a bottle of water and sat on the sofa. "I hope that's all it is."

Frank settled behind his desk. "Okay, so— "

"How's Nikki?"

"Excuse me?"

"The Comptroller. Pregnant, right?"

"Yes, she is."

Sophie smiled. "Is she married?"

Frank shook his head. "That's how it is these days."

Sophie barked a sharp laugh. "It's always been that way."

"Anyway, she's a smart kid. Knows her stuff."

"I hope she likes it here."

"Seems like she does."

Sophie took a sip of water and put the bottle on the end table. "I'm going to talk to her. David seems obsessed with the cash-flow issue—personally, I think he's imagining things—but I may see what she thinks of it."

Frank grabbed the donut but, apparently changing his mind, pushed it to one side. "Let me talk to her about that. I want her to like you."

"I don't care if she likes me. Only that she does her goddam job."

"Then let me do my job," Frank said. "I'll talk to her."

Sophie got up from the sofa and leaned on Frank's desk. "What about tonight?"

"Maybe you should plan ongoing up there alone. I don't think I'll be able to get away, not with all this going on."

Sophie snatched the donut and threw it at Frank's face. He blinked but barely moved, the donut bouncing off his forehead and landing on the credenza behind him.

Frank chuckled.

"I suppose that is a bit funny," Sophie said. "I don't

want to be alone tonight, but you're unavailable."

"Sophie, you know I care about you."

"Not enough, it seems."

16

ASHLEY

MY DAD CAME TO THE HOUSE where I lay on the couch doing nothing but listening to the birds and street noises outside, uninterested in reading, tired of snacking on Trader Joe's banana chips.

"Sweetheart," he said, "what the fuck is going on?"

I sat up and took the bag of banana chips in my hand like it would somehow protect me. "To what are you referring?"

"Joan, your friend. The little asshole showed up over in Ringerton like some God damn Mata Hari, looking like she'd been out all night partying, insulted everyone there, and didn't tell them shit about what's going on."

"Who said she knows anything about what's going on?"

"Everybody there knows she did it. All she has to do is tell them the magic word and all this mess goes away."

"Excuse me?"

He sat down in my one chair and slouched down, exhausted. "We won't press charges if she tells us the magic word."

"You mean like, 'Abracadabra?'"

"What?"

"Isn't 'Abracadabra' the magic word?"

"For fuck's sake, Ashley, what is wrong with you? That's exactly the kind of bullshit Joan pulled in the meeting. Can't you take anything seriously?"

A little buzzer in my brain vibrated. My breathing instantly grew rapid and shallow, and it seemed he was moving away, growing tiny. I clenched my jaws to keep from screaming.

My therapist had a name for this shrinking phenomenon, but I don't recall the term she used. It was the psychological version of running away.

This was how all our interactions had been for the past seven years, since he'd met Sophie after Mom died. He would come into my room, ask me about something he'd just heard about, whether it was my schoolwork, or needing to go to therapy because I cut myself, or that I hadn't done something he wanted me to do. He'd enter with anger. Then he'd get frustrated and would sit down, thinking that would move things forward. Then there'd be confusion, exhaustion, and finally back to anger in some form. Often, indignant outrage made an appearance, and, occasionally, his bruised ego stopped by to say hello.

I understood none of this at first but, over the years, as I worked with counselors, therapists and psychologists, I learned to identify his emotions. I also learned to identify my own, working twice as hard to keep mine in check so that I didn't trigger him, causing an even greater outburst. I hated I had to be the one to do this.

If I so much as hinted that he might need to talk to someone about these feelings, he'd go off on a rant about how being a successful business executive means blah, blah, blah.

That's part of why I left. I had grown tired of psychologically running away, and did it for real.

But there in my rented house, with Dad glaring at me, I felt like that fifteen-year-old girl. After a minute, he threw up his hands, sat back in the chair, and stared at the ceiling.

My therapist's advice came back to me: reset on something routine to bring myself back into the moment and remind him of the boundaries. I grabbed the banana chips and fished out a nice one.

"I don't appreciate being yelled at," I said. "Especially here, where I live."

"Fine. I'm sorry."

I munched on the banana chip. "What sort of magic word are they looking for?"

"The God damn virus encrypted all the machines, and it's looking for some kind of password to decrypt them."

"And they think Joan knows this password?"

"Yes," he said. "It's obvious she did this."

I munched another chip. "I wish I could help."

He rested his elbows on his knees as he leaned forward. "Tell her how fucking serious this is."

"How fucking serious is it?"

"I'm going to lose the business. We've had cash flow

problems for almost a year, in fact. It's a God damn nightmare, like someone has been stealing from us, but I haven't figured out how they're doing it or who it is. Now this happens, and when the banks find out, they'll probably call in the loans. We'll be in bankruptcy court within a week."

"That's pretty serious."

"God damn right it is."

He got up from the chair and reached for the bag of banana chips. I pulled it away.

"What's the big idea?"

"These are mine."

"Everything I've done for you and you won't let me have a couple of crappy potato chips?"

I took a breath and counted to ten, which made me angrier. Counting to ten is terrible advice. It should really be count to two and yell, "Fuck you."

Now I had to take even more time to manage my emotions, and not let them get the better of me. "This is my rental, which I pay with money that Mom bequeathed to me. Could you at least acknowledge that I'm in my place right now?"

"Yes, Sweetheart," he said. "I'm in your place."

"Also, these are not crappy potato chips. They're Trader Joe's banana chips, and they're expensive and I like them a lot. You could ask before trying to shove your hand in the bag."

"I'm sorry."

"Would you like some?"

"Yes, please," he said.

I offered him the bag. He seemed to enjoy them, so I

let him keep it.

"About your embezzler," I said, "maybe whoever's stealing from you is also the person who infected your network."

"What?"

"Like murderers who set fire to a house to destroy evidence. Maybe this person is covering their tracks, using Joan as a convenient patsy to take the fall." This was my desperate attempt to buy more time, but it sounded pretty good when I said it. I think my dad thought so, too.

"Holy shit," he said, spewing small bits of banana chip onto his lap. "I hadn't thought of that."

I went to the kitchen and brought back water for my dad, napkins for his lap, and a fresh bag of banana chips.

"Can I pose another scenario to you?" I asked.

He was still stewing on what I'd said but offered his attention.

"What if you lose the business? Would that be so bad? You could sell the mansion, buy something less expensive. You must have enough money to live without working."

"That's insane. I'm not losing this business. And Sophie would divorce me."

It tempted me to ask, again, if that would be so bad.

"I mean, what would I do?" He wasn't asking, but stating it rhetorically.

"You could spend time with me. We could be a family again."

He was raising a handful of chips to his mouth and

stopped. "Is this about that thing with your mother again?"

"That *thing* with my mother means a lot to me."

"Sweetheart, this is who I am. I can't just stop being me. You have to accept that."

"But you're not being you. You're being who Sophie wants you to be, which is a greedy, money-hungry man who only wants to work to get more money."

He tossed the bag on the coffee table. "You need to grow up and realize that people have to work. Now I wish your mother hadn't left you that money, because you have no motivation to get out and face the world."

"Of course I want to face the world, Dad, but I was giving you one more chance."

"What're you talking about?"

"When I go away to college, or get a job I really care about, it's going to change me. I won't be the girl you used to play with out in the backyard, back when we had an actual family. I've been waiting to grow up all these years, hoping we can connect before it's too late. Before I become someone I have to be, not someone I actually am. But you don't care about that."

"God almighty, Ashley, I've been waiting for you to finally do something. You can't blame who you are on me."

He got up, his face red, and tugged at his collar. "Tell Joan if she's working for someone, she'd better confess now, or it's going to be a lot worse in the end for her."

"What?"

"The embezzler. That's why she wanted the job. She's working with him to cover up the missing money."

"Dad, no. You're missing the point."

"Tell her to confess," he said, and walked out the door.

17

DAVID

David sat at his desk and turned on his laptop. He wanted the problems to be gone, and he didn't care who took them away. If the attacker demanded ransom, he would have paid it by then. He wanted to see the normal startup screen for Windows 10. Instead, he saw the malware's prompt, "magic word?"

David typed, "abracadabra."

The laptop displayed, "magic word?" again.

He tried, "Abracadabra," "Abra Cadabra," and "AbRaCaDaBrA," all to no avail.

He typed, "fuckit," "fuckme," and "fuckyou."

Cassie, his secretary, set a Diet Coke on his desk. "Sorry," she said. "No good news from downstairs."

David nodded.

"They're trying a brutal force approach, or something like that. I ordered pizza and sent Edna out for more pop."

"Maybe I should nail a doubloon to the mast."

"Excuse me?"

David shook his head. "Can you take dictation?"

Cassie grabbed her folio from her desk. "I'm a little rusty, but it should be fine."

Her smile and enthusiasm annoyed David. "Are you having fun?"

"Excuse me?"

"I stand to lose millions of dollars this week. This isn't some team-building exercise."

"Of course," Cassie said. "I'm sorry."

"I'm going to furlough the employees."

"Oh."

"Yeah."

"All the employees?"

David saw the knit of her brow, how she wanted to ask if she, his faithful servant these past twenty years, would also be furloughed. She's a good woman, he thought. She has aged gracefully. Really, she looks as good as ever. She tempted him more than once, and even kept her cool that one time when he kissed her, asking, simply, "What are you doing?" She had earned his every consideration many times over.

David nodded slightly. "This is a serious threat to the business, and I'm not sure what will happen."

Cassie blinked, took a breath and pressed her pen to the paper. "What do you want me to write?"

"Fuck it," David said, and slammed his encrypted, useless laptop shut. "Get that fucker Brian in here."

Brian slumbered in, his eyes bloodshot, the lids drooping, and bags below. His fleece jacket was zipped halfway up, although maybe he'd tried to zip it down and gave up trying.

David noticed, but put out of his mind, the body odor that wafted across the desk as Brian sat down. "Thanks for every—"

Frank rolled in and closed the door in the same motion. He held David's gaze.

Like he owns the place, David thought.

"What'd you want to discuss?" Frank asked. He lowered himself into the other chair, not quite sitting, which would have implied some element of submission. Frank seemed put out. "I've got these guys doing everything possible."

"I need an update," David said. "What progress has been made, what's next, and when are we going to be back in business?"

Brian took a breath and flapped his lips on the exhale, a balloon deflating in the worst way. "We are chasing our tails. We have the brute force password attack going, but there's no telling when, or if, that'll work."

"Brute force?"

Frank slapped the edge of the desk. "They enter every word in the dictionary."

Brian nodded. "It's a dictionary of passwords we found on a white-hat hacking site, words that are used as passwords, and every leet variation, plus numbers."

"That might work?"

"It's been known to," Brian said. "The worst case is if the attacker used a really long, really random password chosen to defy guessing, which would mean a week or more, or never."

"What then?"

Frank slapped the desk. "Plan B."

Brian nodded. "Mike and Oscar are building a decrypting machine, something with a few graphics processors in it, lots of horsepower, the sort of thing crackers would use to break an encryption."

"Can't you buy something like that?" David asked.

"We ordered one, but it won't be here until Wednesday."

"Goddam internet," Frank said.

David thought to ask what Frank meant, but changed his mind. "So Plan B would give us?"

"They might crack the key by Tuesday."

"So, back in business by Wednesday?" David asked.

Brian nodded. He blinked, also, and looked to have fallen asleep for a moment.

"You okay?"

"Need a nap, I think."

Frank snapped his fingers. "We can sleep when we're dead."

David smiled and nodded at Brian, hoping to reassure him. "What about the restore from backups? How's that coming?"

"Ingrid's on that," Frank said. "Good kid. Doing her best."

"So?"

Brian took a breath. "So the backups for the servers are a week old, it turns out. There was a snafu in the system and they hadn't run all week. So it'll be like we were knocked out a week ago, instead of on Friday."

"Fuck."

"Yeah," Frank said. "Fuck."

"It'll take a week to restore all the employee computers," Brain said. "Some of those will have lost a month of data. It's just the nature of backups. You know."

David turned toward Frank. "So we didn't have a viable contingency plan."

"Not for this level of shit," Frank said.

"What level of shit could we have handled?"

Frank slapped the desk. "Do you want to talk about that, or do you want me to get these guys back to work?"

David and Cassie walked down to the second floor. They emerged from the stairwell into the poorly lit office space. It reeked of pizza and stale coffee. To their left, dust floated in the sunlight at the windows.

Across the field of empty cubicles, the glow of desk lamps revealed the location of the I.T. team. Beyond those cubicles, the window shades had been lowered and were outlined by sunlight.

Cassie wrinkled her nose. "I don't think I've ever been down here before."

"I won't be long," David said. "You can head down to the lobby."

David made his way along the outside edge, his legs bathed in the midday light.

Inside the Computer Lab, Ingrid stood at the workbench where laptops were stacked at one end. The rest of the workbench was a mess of equipment and peripherals.

"Excuse me," David said. "I'm sorry to intrude, but I need a favor."

Ingrid looked at him, her face blank as she processed the words. "Okay."

"I'd like a new laptop."

Ingrid nodded, her face brightening with understanding. "Frank told Brian to tell me to focus on restoring the executives. I'm setting them up now, and I'll get the most recent backup—the one from Joan—installed."

"That's fine," David said. "But really, I'd like to take a brand new one for myself, and I'd like that external drive back, if you're done with it."

Ingrid rummaged through some packing material and handed him the drive.

"Does it still have all the data from all the laptops?"

"To be honest, I've done nothing with it yet. Brian told me to focus on the servers."

"That's fine."

"I've been swamped figuring out what backups we have that are valid."

"I understand."

She grabbed a brand new laptop in-the-box from a stack next to the workbench and offered it. "I went to Best Buy last night and bought everything they had. It's close enough to our standard."

"One more thing," David said. "Did you tell anyone about this drive?"

"Not really. Brian is super-focused on the servers."

"Great," David said. "Thank you."

# # # #

DAVID OFFERED CASSIE HIS READING CHAIR IN the corner of his home office. The new laptop had booted up, and he plugged in the printer. "This will just take a minute," he said.

He tidied up his actual desktop, putting bills and some other mail in a folder and dropping that in a drawer. He bookmarked the book he'd been reading and put that on the shelf, then held the chair for Cassie.

"Thank you," she said, and she opened up a blank Word document.

David walked around the desk and stared at his bookshelves, pondering how to begin the memorandum. "People may not even know what has happened," he said.

"What's all this?" Sophie asked. She stood in the doorway, holding her glasses above her eyes with one hand, gripping a drink in the other.

"I need to get a memo out to the employees," David said.

"Frank told me you haven't been helpful."

"What the hell is he talking about?"

"Well?" Sophie asked. "Have you?"

"This happened on his watch on his team."

"Thanks to that little stupid friend of Ashley's," Sophie said. "Tell me, are you sleeping with her?"

David held his breath.

"Oh relax," Sophie said. "I know you're not capable, but Frank was angry and wondered."

"Excuse us," David said to Cassie.

He escorted Sophie out of the office and down the hall towards the rec room. "What in the name of God are you insinuating? And in front of Cassie?"

"Sorry, but did I make her jealous?"

"Okay," David said. "What is this shit?"

"I'm frustrated," Sophie said. "You know none of this would have happened if you'd taken the company public like Frank recommended. We could have put legitimate practices in place, had a proper CIO, and we'd have ten times the wealth right now."

"This is not the time to bring up that load of bull."

"You have to admit we wouldn't be in this situation if you'd listened to Frank."

"Where the hell is this coming from?"

"Tell me why she's here, in my house?"

"Cassie? Because we don't have a working system in the entire building. I can't even email the staff. We're going to write a memo and take it to OfficeMax to make copies so I can hand them out in the morning."

Sophie sipped her drink. "I believe that's what my first husband would have called 'bush league.'"

"For God's sake, Sophie. Don't you care anything about what has happened?"

"Of course I care, David. You're my husband. I know how it pains you to be in this position. Still, I can't help thinking how it was your well-meaning, but tragic, devotion to your daughter that led you to honor her strange request to hire her friend. It was that Joan person who caused this entire mess. It comes back to you, doesn't it, dear?"

"Oh, that's just lovely," David said. "Listen: Frank demanded—no, begged—for control of I.T., yet he failed to install a professional contingency plan. I'm in charge of engineering and those processes have never failed. But it doesn't matter how this started. How Frank's team responds is what matters, and if we don't solve the problem soon, I'll be forced to take drastic steps."

Sophie rattled the ice cubes in her drink. "I'm headed into the office now. Anything you want me to tell him?"

"I trust you'll keep our discussions confidential."

"Of course, David dear. Pillow talk is between us."

18

Shame compelled David to take the memo to OfficeMax and make the copies himself. He used the self-serve machines, rather than hand it to the clerk behind the counter, to account for absolutely every copy.

He understood the story would be out there soon enough, not that it was newsworthy compared to other scandals and disasters befalling the world. It was that he wanted to tell the employees himself.

Email would have been fine, but that required people to come into the office and use their workstations. Most of the factory staff didn't even have a computer.

The solution was to get them printed and meet them outside, in front of the building. Gather them around, tell them about the problem, and give them the furlough memo so that there would be no misunderstanding about pay. He'd have to call Tanessa, the union steward, tonight. There was something in the contract about giving two weeks of notice, so he'd rely on the force majeure clause to send them home.

No reason to publicly admit how tight money was. A

few people would guess, but there'd be plenty of rumors battling for attention over the next few days.

David carried the box containing the 400 copies to his Chrysler and set them on the passenger seat. He started the car and blasted the air conditioning, opening the sunroof to let out the heat, and waited. There was so much to do, but he didn't know where to start.

He texted Cassie, "Any progress?"

He needed to tell Sophie to call Karen, the human resources specialist, and tell her to be on the call when they broke the news to Tanessa.

He needed to eat something other than donuts.

He needed to look into the money irregularities.

He needed to guess the secret word.

Cassie texted, "Nope. No progress. Sorry."

It was late in the afternoon in the parking lot at the Arborland Shopping Plaza. Thick traffic on Washtenaw Avenue stutter-stepped. Heat waves rose between the cars in the lot. He could pick up food, maybe drive out to the Arb and visitF the peaceful gardens. He could go to a nice restaurant, enjoy the quiet of between-meal eating. He could watch a baseball game while eating at a bar.

Nothing seemed right, so he got back on I-94 and drove toward Ringerton. As he approached the exit, he recalled the drive with Heather almost thirty years prior, shortly before they were married, when they came here to inspect the place where they'd be working.

He hadn't thought of Heather in any significant way for quite a while. Recently, she'd come up as part of the discourse with Ashley, and had served as a prop, mostly. In that discourse—arguments, really—Heather wasn't the person he once loved, but the reason he was still fighting with his daughter nearly eight years after Heather died.

The Shell gas station passed on his right. The combination KFC/Taco Bell, looped by cars, passed on the left. Ringerton Road was quiet after that. Two vacant buildings stood as sentries before the bridge crossing Belle Creek.

The downtown area—a half-mile strip of the same road—was lined with buildings built after World War II, when the population shift made the town viable. When David and Heather first saw it, crossing the bridge as he had just done, they were smitten by the run-down authenticity of the banks, hardware shops, and grocery stores re-purposed as cafes, coffee shops, and vintage clothing stores.

Two taverns at the center of the strip were the real-deal, serving drinks for over seventy years.

The buildings along the far end of the downtown strip gave off a vibe of stubborn hopefulness. Artisan repurposed the store fronts as paper shops, financial consultants, and purveyors of soap. The last two buildings, facing each other across the street, were tattoo parlors catering to hard-core bikers, wannabe Detroit rockers, and millennial hipsters.

The Sinclair sign at the out-of-business filling station marked the beginning of the residential area, with street after street of bungalows, ranches, and up-and-down duplexes. He reflexively turned left down their old street and slowed to a stop at their first house.

He and Heather had rented the upstairs unit. It was

warm and airy. It had access to the finished attic and a balcony on the back. They didn't have access to the garage until they bought the house and moved themselves downstairs.

Heather had spearheaded many upgrades, repairs, and refurbishment projects. By the time Ashley was born, the two units were recombined into a single home. They added a room on the back and modernized the bathrooms.

It seemed their forever home.

Even when the business grew exponentially, and they had the money to buy the entire block, Heather insisted they stay there in the same house. The only change was to rebuild the detached garage and add a studio apartment above it for guests, or whatever.

The studio became the place Heather's parents stayed while she slowly died of cancer.

A car honked from behind and David waved it around. He wasn't aware how long he'd been stopped on the street.

He drove out of the residential area towards the light industrial park, home to HD Enterprises. He drove past the industrial park entrance and toward the older part of town.

In that corner of the city was the original downtown, where Ringerton Road crossed Route 12. Turn left and you head for Detroit. Turn right and you head for Chicago.

Once decrepit Victorian houses—refurbished and upgraded to better than the original quality—lined both roads, six or seven in each direction, home to the bed-

and-breakfast proprietors and wealthier residents. Directly on the corner were single-story buildings: a cafe, a bakery, a coffee shop, and a supper club that was only open for evening meals on the weekend.

He absently turned on Columbia and drove until Lake Ringerton come into view. He turned and drove along the shore, back toward the bridge. As he approached the city's main road, he saw the cemetery where Heather was buried across the water. Rather than heading straight toward the highway, he took the road leading to the bridge to the cemetery.

As David made his way from the car, two men dug a grave, likely for a funeral the next day. One man operated a backhoe, its diesel engine chugging out black smoke, while the other man leaned on a spade and watched.

It was late in the afternoon. David felt the sun on his face. Sweat ran down his neck. His shirt was damp and clung to his skin. He didn't like the idea of returning to the office, soaked in sweat, facing the prospect of an all-nighter. He'd need to freshen up before greeting his employees in the morning to tell them to go back home.

The workman leaning on the spade glanced at David, who felt the heat of shame in his face as he wasn't sure where the grave was. He recalled the day of the burial and recognized a tree, which led him to Heather.

The marker's left side was inscribed:

Heather Rice
Beloved Daughter, Wife, Mother

The right side was inscribed:

David Rice

David stared at the gravestone but felt nothing. Was that even his name? He'd been devastated, but now he couldn't recall the pain. Was that it? Was it normal to feel nothing once enough time had passed?

The backhoe's engine went silent. The two men walked toward their pickup truck parked on the road as a breeze cooled David's skin.

A robin alighted on the nearest tree and sang, "Trill-a-dee, trill-a-dee."

Two starlings darted past, swooping low over the grass and quickly leaving the area.

David thought of the first time he'd met Heather. He was at the Undergraduate Library—the "ugly"—studying for the Mechanics mid-term. She sat down at his table and opened the same textbook. They exchanged a nod, and both continued their study.

An hour later, his attention flagged. The young lady at the table passed him a note, asking about the answer to one of the practice problems. David wrote his solution on the back of the note. She marked it up and passed it back, correcting his mistake, but adding a question mark.

He nodded. She was right.

"Do you want to get coffee?" he had whispered.

When she nodded, he had asked her name.

The memory left him as a strong gust of wind swept across the gravestones. He wiped a tear from his eye.

David squatted and touched a hand to the ground. "Heather," he said, answering the question he'd posed so many years ago.

He could have sworn he heard her say, "David."

19

Back at the office, David doodled around the corners of the paper as he sat at his desk. At the top, in the middle, he'd written: "heather."

Below it, on each successive line, he'd tried a variation:

heather

HEATHER

Heath3r

None of them worked.

He doodled a scene at the bottom of the page, his personal hack for thinking, moving the pencil back and forth, and the shape of a leafy tree top emerged. He added the trunk, some grass, a horizon, and more trees. He drew three squiggle-lines to represent the starlings. He added a headstone and the form of a fresh grave in the tree's shade.

rehtaeh

H347h3r

Had any of them worked, David would have been annoyed. Ashley had told him how her mother spoke to her at the grave. That he remembered Heather's voice did not mean she was talking to him.

In fact, magical thinking was a pet peeve for both of them. Heather, in particular, despised it. They were engineers. They liked to figure out why things happened, especially when it seemed magic was involved.

"Any sufficiently advanced science or technology seems like magic to the ignorant," someone had quipped. And that person had been correct.

You give in to a belief in magic, or superstition, and you give up on science. David was not about to do that.

He hadn't launched a fifty-million dollar business with magical thinking.

The systems would crack the password soon enough, and then they'd get the business back.

He was reminded of the first time Ashley had asked to use the computer at the house to play a game. He'd been against it, but Heather convinced him otherwise.

"I don't want Ashley deleting any of our files," he had said.

"She'll use my account."

"You don't even tell me your password."

"Fine," she said. "It's fairly odd parents, lower case, with a zero for the O."

"Fairly odd parents?"

"The cartoon we watch with Ashley every day. She

loves it."

"She'll remember that?"

"It's on a Post-it note stuck to the monitor."

Now he could picture the note, the password written in Heather's block letters with serifs and flares borrowed from cursive applied liberally, and a stroke through the zero to differentiate it from the letter O:

fairly0ddparents

He entered it into the ransomware's challenge on his infected laptop and the program began decrypting the files, listing its progress and scrolling the recovered filenames faster than he could read them.

David felt a tingle of electricity blast out from his spine to his hands, his feet, and across his head.

Later that afternoon, Frank came into David's office. "The man, the myth, the legend," he said. "How'd you do it?"

David glanced but wasn't interested in talking with Frank. He watched the listing of recovered files scroll across the laptop's screen as the ransomware decrypted the hard drive.

Frank opened the mini-fridge, but it was empty. "What the heck? Where's the wine? Don't you have wine?"

David shook his head.

"I thought we should celebrate. It's not every day you save the company from the brink of disaster. I'll go get some champagne, unless you want something stronger?"

The ransomware was 90% done. It was mind-boggling how many files were on his tiny laptop. "I'm fine."

"You okay?" Frank asked. "Heroes are usually a little more upbeat than this."

Brian stood in the doorway and knocked. "You wanted me?"

Frank waved him in as he planted his right cheek on the corner of David's desk. "What's the what? When will we be good to go?"

Brian stood before the desk and referred to his padfolio. "The servers will be done by eight. The laptops and desktops will all be done by morning. If you want, we can open for business, but we'd like to run an anti-virus on everything, check for any lingering malware or back doors. So maybe delay for an hour?"

David fixed his gaze on Brian. "We're going to close tomorrow. Suspend normal business operations. Once you get everything started today, you can send folks home, let them sleep. Take tomorrow to do whatever you need, clean up, and maybe think about better processes."

"What're you talking about?" Frank asked.

"Brian's team needs to rest. We need to ensure that this won't happen again."

"We pay them a pretty good salary," Frank said. "It's okay to make them work."

David rested his hands on the desk. He heard his heart beat, felt the warmth in his cheeks. This was a bossy moment. He didn't enjoy being the boss—too many business decisions, not enough time engineering solutions—but it was his row to hoe.

"Alright fine," Frank said. "Maybe you're right."

"I appreciate it," Brian said. "I think the team will, too."

Frank slapped Brian on the shoulder and steered him to the door. "They better be bright eyed and bushy tailed tomorrow."

Frank closed the office door and settled in the chair across from David. "Well?"

"You have something you wish to discuss?" David asked.

"Cut the crap," Frank said. "How'd you figure out the password?"

"Don't worry about it."

Frank chuckled. "It was Joan, right? You were banging her, something pissed her off, and she did it to get revenge. But you finally guessed her password."

"It's offensive that you even think that."

"Hey man, she was a little hottie. And she dressed like she wanted it. Am I right?"

"Stop it, Frank," David said. "You've crossed several lines already, you have your own problems around here to take care of, and talking shit out of your ass won't help."

Frank gave a low, guttural growl. "Don't tell me you actually like the little cutie. I think Sophie would put up with a side chick, but you can't fall for her. That's just asking for—"

"Get out." David stood up and punched the desk. "Get out before I fire your ass."

Frank heaved a sigh and went to the door. "My apologies. I thought we understood each other, but I was wrong."

# # # #

DAVID RETURNED TO HIS HOUSE AND DROPPED his briefcase in his office. He paused in the hallway and listened to the murmur of Sophie's voice on the phone upstairs in her room.

He crossed to the other side and went inside Ashley's room. It had been nearly two years since Ashley moved out, and she'd stayed there a handful of times since then, usually around the holidays. The bookshelf was as she left it. The layer of dust was the only thing added.

He found the yearbooks lying flat on the bottom shelf as if put there, rather than shelved. Each volume still had the purchase receipt inside and creaked when he opened them as if for the first time. Joan Naumov was there in the seventh, eighth, and ninth-grade yearbooks, but missing in the next two.

Ashley didn't have a yearbook for what would have been her senior year because she had stopped going. The ninth grade yearbook would have to do.

He took it back to his home office and retrieved the eight-by-ten-inch printed photo of Joan he'd gotten from Vince in Security before leaving. That ninth grader had grown up quite a bit. Her nose, cheeks and chin were all different. What bothered him was that he couldn't remember ever meeting this Joan.

He'd been so busy, once he and Sophie married and moved in together in Ann Arbor, that he didn't question much about Ashley's time with her friend. He was simply relieved that she had any friends at all.

Ashley's quitting school had robbed them of the normal activities around senior year, commencement, and the progression of parties during the summer. Instead, he'd been worried sick about her. She threatened to file for emancipation. Finally, the job at Britney's coffee shop settled things down. Eighteen months later, Ashley got her GED and went to community college.

Throughout those tumultuous years, Ashley mentioned Joan as her best friend. Joan helped her find a place to stay. Joan helped her shop for food and clothing. Ashley and Joan studied for the GED together.

At first, David blamed Joan for Ashley's delinquency. Ashley explained how Joan was her better half, and David worried they were in a relationship. But they both went to community college, kept working at the coffee shop, and made it seem like things would work out. Of course, he'd give Joan a job. He'd have given her a suitcase full of cash in gratitude for being Ashley's friend.

Sophie opened the office door without knocking. "You are here."

David closed the yearbook on Joan's photo and set it aside on his desk. "What's up?"

"I spoke with Frank."

"Oh?"

Sophie strolled over to the desk and leaned down to

look at the yearbook. "Feeling nostalgic?"

"Why did you call Frank?"

"He called me to discuss the shut down for tomorrow. And by the way, when were you going to inform me? As Chief Operating Officer, I may have had some say in the matter, darling."

"I came home to discuss it with you."

"Of course you did..."

Sophie flipped open the yearbook and took hold of the photo of Joan. "I didn't believe Frank when he said it, but do you have a crush on this child?"

"What, exactly, did Frank say?"

"Oh relax," Sophie said. She strolled to the reading corner and sat in the chair. "If anything, I think Frank is jealous. You have to admit, the little minx is something of a femme fatale."

"She's Ashley's friend."

Sophie smiled. "Just like in the movie with what's his name."

"Stop it. I've never even met her."

"You seem obsessed now."

"God damn it, just stop. I'm trying to be serious."

"Of course, darling."

"Have you ever met this Joan?"

"No. Haven't you?"

"I was trying to remind myself, but I'm coming up blank."

Sophie strolled back to the desk and studied the picture again. "I'd have remembered her. I wonder what she saw in Ashley. No offense, David, but Ashley must fade to nothing in the glare of this one. Perhaps

Ashley was smitten, like you?"

David closed the yearbook on the picture again and put it in his desk drawer. "I'm going to go talk to Ashley."

"You think she had something to do with this ransomware mess?"

"No." David grabbed his briefcase and waited for Sophie to leave the office. "I'm hoping she can help us find Joan, though."

"You think Joan did this, then."

"No," David said. "I don't know that."

"Frank thinks we should hire a private investigator," Sophie said. "He suggests we get a look at her financial records. Someone probably paid her to do what she did."

"We don't know she did anything wrong."

Sophie smiled. "Methinks you're protesting a lot."

David let out a weary sigh. "It still might just be Jared, like she suggested."

Sophie laughed. "Then how was it you were able to guess the password?"

"Someone may have hacked into my systems and found some reference to it."

"Doesn't sound likely."

"I'm not drawing any conclusions until we have more data."

Sophie patted his shoulder. "There's the engineer. So cute."

20

ASHLEY

I HAD ORDERED DOORDASH, SO I was confused when the knock on the door turned out to be my dad. I was so hungry for actual food, had waited all day to eat a meal, too distracted and anxious to look for anything to eat beyond the basket where I kept chips, crackers and nuts.

What I'm saying is that I wasn't prepared to deal with my dad, despite knowing he might show up, eventually.

"I need a favor," he said. He stepped past me into the front room. "Actually, I need your help."

I leaned out the door: the street was empty. "Okay."

He settled into the chair and waited. I could tell he wanted me to sit on the sofa, but I wanted to wait by the door. I was that hungry.

"Have you heard we guessed the password?"

I shook my head.

"It was a password you know. Or at least you used to use it."

"Small world."

"How did that happen?" he asked. "How did a password that your mother used on our family computer, and which you used to play a game on that computer, come to decrypt all the computers at my business?"

I abandoned my post at the front door and sat on the sofa. My head was a little foggy and the sharp edges in his voice told me he was not amused by this discovery.

"Did you put Joan up to this?"

"Kind of," I said.

"I'm going to have to speak with Joan. You know that, right?"

"I don't think that can happen."

"This is a serious matter. "

"Joan understands how serious it is."

"Two dozen people have worked around the clock because of this. We're shutting down the business tomorrow and possibly more days. We're spending tens of thousands because of this and will lose tens of thousands more in revenue. We avoided disaster only because I guessed the password. Do you want to tell me what's going on?"

A car pulled into the driveway. You'd think I wouldn't have an appetite at a moment like that, but my mouth watered when the car door opened. "Someone's coming."

"So let them come," my dad said. "You owe me some answers."

He was talking like an angry dad on a television show. I was suddenly angry that he was playing a part, rather than talking to me. Or yelling at me. He couldn't even show any genuine emotion.

There were footsteps on the porch and a knock on the door. "Leave it outside, please."

The delivery guy said, "Okay," and made his retreat.

I thought I smelled the ramen bowl with tofu but it was in my head, of course.

My dad lifted his hands and dropped them back in his lap. "This is ridiculous."

"You broke your promise."

"That?"

"Yes."

"You tried to destroy our business because of something I agreed to when I was overcome with grief."

"It was a promise."

He shook his head. "I loved your mother very much. I was trying to ease her pain. I didn't want her to worry about the future."

I got my ramen bowl from the front door, scrounged for a clean fork in the kitchen, and returned to the sofa. I didn't want to eat there with my dad watching, but I'd only eaten there, on my sofa, for the past two years. So I ate.

I didn't enjoy the food. My heart beat wildly with rage. With each noodle I slurped into my mouth, the pressure in my head ticked upward. A dozen different memories jumbled together in my brain, a ramen bowl of emotion.

How do you even talk to someone who so casually admits to lying to their wife on her deathbed? How do you deal with that when it's your father?

"Are you just going to sit there slurping your soup?"

he asked.

It was a ramen bowl, but that wasn't the point. I could only think of one way to get through to him. "I did it."

"You did what?"

I slurped a mouthful of soup and sucked a noodle into my mouth. "The ransomware. I did it."

He nodded, tapped his right fist on the chair's arm. "You put Joan up to this."

I set the ramen bowl on a precarious pile of paperbacks. "I'm Joan."

He leaned forward. "What?"

"I'm Joan. Joan is me. I went to HD Enterprises, found all the weaknesses, and installed the ransomware."

"But Joan is someone else. She's your friend."

"My friend Joan moved away years ago. I follow her Insta, but we haven't talked or anything."

He stood up and looked around, searching for something but unable to recall what he'd misplaced. Finally, he moved in front of me. "That's insane."

Not liking that word, I picked up my ramen bowl and began slurping.

"If what you say is true..." He looked around the room for something. "Do you have any idea how many laws you broke? How much money you cost me?"

While holding the bowl in one hand, I used my other hand to pull the wig off of my head and removed my eyeglass frames, removing all doubt that I had been Joan.

"For the love of God," my father said.

I lifted the bowl to my mouth and slurped.

"What the hell am I supposed to do with this?"

I couldn't help it but, as I was about to say 'sorry,' I burped.

"Why did you even tell me?"

"Same reason you told me you lied to mom, on her deathbed, about the promise to take care of me."

He paced across the room and settled back into the chair. "These are not the same things," he said. "Mine was done in an act of mercy for someone I loved. Yours is an unlawful act…a cyber-crime that jeopardized hundreds of jobs. How can you possibly equate the one with the other?"

"The specific acts are different, sure."

His head twitched, and he fluttered his hands. "Okay. So?"

"But you told me about your violation of a sacred trust with someone I held more dearly than life. You lied to my mother and now you callously tell me about it, admitting to never intending to keep the promise you made. I told you how I violated something you hold more dearly than life: your company, and the money it brings to you. I loved Mom the way you love money. You hurt Mom, so I hurt your money."

"That makes no sense."

"It does," I said, "but you're going to need some time to work it out. It took me these past few years to realize how much money means to you. I mean, I thought it was Sophie, and maybe the spell would break and you'd remember me, but that didn't happen. Finally, I came to terms that it was money all along. Maybe now you'll realize that the promise you made to Mom meant that much to me."

He covered his face with his hands and rocked back and forth in the chair. He took a breath and said, "Okay, I admit I broke the promise, but you just don't understand how critical it is to stay focused on a business..."

I slurped up the last of the ramen and took the bowl to the kitchen.

"You should go, Dad. I don't care if you call the police, or sue me, or whatever it is big bad businessmen do when they've been wronged by the world."

He stood, but seemed confused.

"I wasn't going to let the business collapse," I said. "I gave you the backup copies of those laptops. They would have recovered in a couple of days. Or I would have told you the magic word. I was hoping you'd realize that things could change in the blink of an eye."

"You're not making sense," he said.

"I don't care. I'm going to bed, so please close the door when you leave."

21

DAVID

Vince, the security guy, hailed David as he entered the building. "Sophie asked me to call her when you arrived. You want me to do that?"

David, lost in thought at the moment, hesitated, not understanding. "Who?"

"Your wife, the Chief Operating Officer, Sophie Fox. She asked me to let her know when you arrived."

David nodded in understanding, then shook his head. "No. I'll go find her myself. And thank you."

Vince raised his thumb in acknowledgment.

On the top floor, Cassie noticed him as he stepped off the elevator. She stood and watched him approach.

"Everything all right?" he asked.

"Sophie has been in a meeting with Frank to discuss the shutdown."

"Okay."

"They seemed concerned that you weren't answering your phone."

"I was with my daughter."

Cassie smiled. "How is she?"

"Fine," he said, but hurried into his office to drop his things.

David used the side door in his office to cross through the conference room into Sophie's office. The door, however, was locked.

"Sophie?"

Frank opened the door. "There he is."

David stepped inside. Sophie was at her desk, which was covered in papers. Jared sat across from her and Frank made his way to the other chair where, apparently, he'd been sitting.

This had been Heather's office many years before. David hadn't thought of it that way since Sophie moved in. David avoided the space entirely while Sophie had it remodeled. This hadn't been a conscious act, like he was repulsed because Sophie was destroying Heather's space. Rather, there had been a lot of dust, noise and workers, so he avoided it entirely, spending his time down a floor with the engineers, or holed up in his office, eventually moving to the home office.

He hadn't even thought to retrieve Heather's mementos from this office. How had he let go of her so quickly?

It came back in a burst of memory: Heather at the desk, which was covered with the pads of large paper she preferred for capturing her ideas. A laptop on one side was used in bursts of energy to build models or plan projects. White boards covered two walls, and huge Post-It notes covered the white boards, creating layers of ideas depicted in notes and sketches. Heather was the only person smarter than David in their world, and she had been the driving force behind much of their success.

Since she'd died, they'd had no particular innovation of engineering. Sophie introduced efficiencies in manufacturing, growth of their markets, and pressured suppliers for discounts, all of which led to financial success. Lately, the financial success was shrinking, trending toward zero.

So what had Sophie and Frank been discussing just now?

"Is everything alright, Darling?" Sophie asked. "You look as if you've seen a ghost."

David nodded. "Tired, I guess."

"Shall we go into the conference room?" Frank asked. "I can catch you up on things."

David shook his head. "Computer recovery progressing?"

"On schedule," Frank said. "Most of the nerds have left. Brian and Ingrid are staying behind to observe, but I think Brian is asleep somewhere."

"Fine."

"If we're closed for business tomorrow," Sophie said, "I think it's fair that we don't pay anyone. Cash flow is tight, as you know."

"I'll cover payroll from our personal accounts," David said.

"Excuse me?"

"Everyone gets paid, even if the company can't afford it."

Frank chuckled. "There's no need for that. We have a line of credit if needed. I mean, it'll be tight, but we should be fine."

"It won't be fine," Sophie said. "If they aren't working, they shouldn't get paid."

David took another look around the office. "Everyone gets paid. Let me know if we're short."

# # # #

DAVID AND CASSIE REVISED THE MEMO TO distribute in the morning. While Cassie delivered a printed copy of the memo to Sophie and Frank, David called the union representative directly to explain the situation.

When Cassie returned, Sophie was behind her with the memo in one hand and a can of Diet Coke in the other.

Sophie set the can on David's desk and cracked it open. "Cassie, be a dear and get me a glass and some ice."

"I know you're concerned," David said. "I promise we're going to have better days."

"You'll hear me out though, right?" To Cassie, she said, "That'll be all, dear."

"Hang on," David said. "Cassie, stay."

Sophie got a bottle of rum from the cabinet. She paused before pouring. "The ice, dear?"

"There isn't any," Cassie said.

"Then go to my office."

"Hang on," David said. "I need Cassie to call all the managers so they're not surprised in the morning, and ask them to reach out to as many employees as possible."

"Oh fine," Sophie said. "The cola is cold."

Sophie watched Cassie leave, then shifted in her seat to fully face David. "Honestly, David, you worry me. I think you should go see a doctor."

"I'm fine."

Sophie poured out the rum and topped it with the cola. "You seem different. Has this cyber-attack unnerved you?"

"I've been forced to look at things from another point of view."

"But why are you giving away more of our money? This weekend has been expensive with nothing to show for it. You've been worried about cash flow for months. Now you seem absolutely reckless."

Several of Frank's accounting practices could be classified as reckless, but Sophie would argue the points, and he'd get nowhere. She had the gift of contrariness, willing to disagree and dispute any assertions made. David had learned this was Sophie's siege tactic for winning a battle, starving your argument like it was Stalingrad, until you surrendered by changing the subject. "I'm going to look into the cash flow problem myself. At least the ransomware didn't demand an actual ransom. We'd really be in a state, then."

Sophie uncrossed her arms as she crossed her legs. "Too bad you didn't think of the magic word on Friday. We could have gone to the party at the Henderson's estate. Half of Dexter was there—the good half."

David nodded. "Are we ready from a human resources perspective on the furlough?"

Sophie sipped her drink. "You're paying everyone, so what's to do? It's more of an ad hoc holiday. I may not come in myself. I think I deserve a paid holiday, same as everyone."

"Fine. I'll see you at home."

"Are you trying to get rid of me?"

"I want to work on something, so yes."

Sophie smiled and stood up. "I knew you were a hardworking man and a faithful provider when I met you. That's why I married you."

David smiled, but he wasn't feeling it.

"Frank wants to get moving on tracking down Joan. Just wanted to make you aware."

"No," David said. "I don't want him to pursue it."

"Now I know you're not yourself," Sophie said. "That little bitch nearly destroyed us."

"I don't want us wasting any more time or effort on that. We have to get past the attack and move forward."

"Frank may pursue her on his own. Of course, he may just want to take the little minx on a date."

"Tell Frank to secure our I.T. processes. If he won't, I will."

"The processes served us well for years because we trusted our employees. It was you who vouched for Joan."

And just like that, she trapped him in an argument that could go on for hours if he allowed it. "I'm done with this, so please excuse me."

"Ooh," Sophie said. "I love it when you talk dirty."

David glanced at her, but returned his focus to the spreadsheet on his laptop.

"You're serious about this?" Sophie asked.
David nodded. "I'll see you at home."

22

DAVID

DAVID THOUGHT ABOUT WHAT HE NEEDED to do next and wondered if he could still trust the laptop decrypted and scrubbed by I.T. Something was amiss with the cash flow. Ashley had attacked with ransomware. He didn't think she would have done anything else on purpose, but if she downloaded a hackers kit, other nefarious software may have gone undetected.

That she could pull off the attack proves that they had been vulnerable for years, and there could be software installed stealing money from them, siphoning funds, or any number of covert acts to steal information. He'd be crazy to use his compromised laptop to do the research needed.

He checked if his laptop still offered a hidden, password-free share of the hard drive. He'd spoken directly with Ingrid and gotten the explanation on how to use it and remove it, if it still existed.

He drilled into the Control Panel, found the Computer Administration applet, and interrogated the shares: nothing there.

Curious, he tried to access Sophie's and Frank's laptops. Both requests were denied, which was a good thing.

An engineer at heart, he took an engineer's approach to the problem.

First, the problem was that the financial statements didn't feel right compared to the sales figures over the past two years. It was like an engine losing oil, but there was no visible leak. If you find a puddle on the garage floor, you know what you're dealing with. With no evidence of how the oil escapes, assume it's leaking into the cylinders and being burned up like fuel.

Okay, so you have to look at the rate of loss. He'd track down the official financial statements Frank provided the past three years, then dig into the ledger.

Of course, he could ask Frank to do this, but Frank was adamant that everything was balanced, and that David need only dig into the details to understand. Every time he'd attempted to do this—admittedly, it had only been three times the past year—something came up, and the meeting was delayed.

David suggested an outside auditor two months prior. Sophie had laughed, saying it was a waste of money. They could all look at the ledger spreadsheet together, and then he'd see how it added up.

That would have satisfied David, but it hadn't happened.

A year ago, David thought it was his problem in not understanding something about their financial situation, about how there was less income, and more expenses, than he thought.

Six months ago, he wondered if Frank had a strange accounting practice, a technique that moved money around the ledger for some tax advantage. Again, David need only understand what was happening.

Today, for the first time, he wondered if Frank might be doing something untoward. David was loath to think that Frank would steal from them—he was paying Frank almost three hundred thousand dollars a year, plus a substantial share of the profit—but today David's world was rattled.

Learning that Ashley had been living an alternate personality for the past two weeks, and possibly the past five years, becoming her own imaginary friend, made David doubt everything.

If it was remotely possible for Frank to be stealing from him, he certainly couldn't trust Frank to disprove it.

And then there was Sophie, his wife of eight years, who had recruited Frank to join the company and had entrusted him with her faith and the financial future of their hundred million dollar a year business. It was insane to consider, but what if something was happening between them?

David chose not to think any more about that. He would simply look at the data.

David munched on Fritos and sipped a Diet Coke as Windows restored the backup of Frank's laptop . It reminded him of college, when he and Heather survived on pop and chips, or so it seemed.

"David," Sophie called from outside the office.

He went to the door and stepped out, offering Sophie a Frito.

"For the love of God, no," she said. "Frank and I are going to find some place in Ann Arbor to eat."

"Is that an invitation?"

"Of course, David. Someone has to pick up the check."

He shook the bag of Fritos. "I'm good."

"Seriously," Sophie said. "We all deserve something decent to eat. Tomorrow's a day off, so we'll have drinks. You know how delightful Ann Arbor is in July, with the desperate students gone. It'll just be us, the squirrels, and a few homeless persons."

"You have fun."

Sophie plucked a single chip from the bag and licked it. She wrinkled her nose and dropped it back in the bag. "Disgusting."

David started in the Documents folder and found a sub-folder named "ledgers-final." Within that were folders named for the previous eight years, the same number of years Frank had been with the company.

In each of those folders was a collection of spreadsheets that created their bookkeeping system. There was one called "chart-of-accounts.xslx," another called "income-and-expense.xslx," and another called "financial-statements.xslx." That was the basic bookkeeping system Heather created years ago, when they launched the business and realized they needed to keep track of things.

They hired a bookkeeper, who helped them set up

"payroll.xslx" and a couple of others. Before the end of that year, as sales continued, and they realized their taxes were going to be complicated beyond their combined knowledge, they made arrangements with a CPA and turned over all payroll to a third-party vendor.

For a dozen years, it went smoothly like that. They hired a second bookkeeper, a Comptroller, and someone to worry about taxes. They hired their own CPA and added financial analysts, but the basic bookkeeping system remained the same. They hired an accounting firm to audit their books to assure themselves all was well.

Shortly before Heather got sick, they had started down a path of using a dedicated system to manage the ledgers and all transactions, but her illness interrupted that work.

Sophie had, at first, ingratiated herself with David as a financial consultant and reviewed accounting practices. After they were married, he suggested she would take it over entirely. Instead, Sophie convinced David to hire Frank, who had a decade of experience as a chief financial officer.

Frank talked about modernizing the finance department, finding investors for additional growth, and eventually taking the company public. David wasn't terribly interested in going public, but he had noticed a slight dampening of his interest in the business operations. A public offering would allow him to step away while keeping his fortune, and possibly growing it more quickly.

Although sales increased steadily, profits dwindled. Not a lot. A few percentage points each year. Frank pointed to increased expenses and suggested various cost saving moves. He hired a less expensive CPA and found an auditing firm that charged half as much as the previous one.

Sophie trumpeted Frank's ideas about taking the company public. Access to the stock exchange, she suggested, would make all these petty problems disappear.

David chuckled as he sipped his Diet Coke. Could it really be that simple?

23

ASHLEY

I'D BEEN AWAKE SINCE FOUR O'CLOCK thinking about my mother. That was a thing I did a lot of since she died. I'd try to remember times with her and re-live it in my mind, focusing on those moments, trying to bring her back to me.

The problem is that, when you're a little kid, you hardly pay attention to your parents. You're more interested in who ignored you at school, what the other kids are doing and, if you're lucky, being with another kid. Of course, you want to be with your parents, but you take them for granted.

You certainly don't pay enough attention to figure out what they wore, said, and ate ten years later. None of that goes into deep memory.

I caught a tiny break because my dad bought fancy cameras every few months, constantly upgrading from one to another, Canon, Fuji, Nikon and Leica, then starting over again. He took photos of me and Mom doing whatever; back then, we were his entire world. He was learning how to be a photographer by taking photos and filled up the family computer with thousands of images. So I could literally picture her in all of those situations, from the mundane to the exotic, and see what she ate most of the time, as well.

We drove out to the zoo in Battle Creek, once, and she's wearing a purple Life is Good T-shirt, tan Capri slacks and those canvas sneakers with three grommets. She has a little purse slung cross-wise across her chest. She has sunglasses but they're pushed up on her head, lifting her blond hair, which escapes in wisps.

She and I smile at the camera. The smiles look sincere, like we're having a good time.

I know we ate a huge, hot pretzel and dipped it in melted cheese. That's what I remember: eating a pretzel.

We drank pop through straws in paper cups.

We stood on the platform overlooking the African Savannah display, and a giraffe's head is next to ours, its tongue reaching for the leaves on the tree overhanging the platform.

It's hard, almost impossible, to conjure the actual memory, other than the pretzel. What I remember is the picture I memorized, and some early memory of what we might have said, what made us laugh, and how we came to choose a pretzel for a snack. I remember giving the giraffe a name, but I'm not certain that's an actual memory or something I invented while looking at the photos on the computer.

I don't know what to do with knowing the memory may be invented, but cherishing it because it helps me remember my dead mother.

Britney came to my house mid-morning. "I'm here to beg you for help."

I was in the backyard, watching the birds feed, still thinking of my mom.

Britney sat beside me in the grass. "Are you okay?"

"What have you heard?"

"Nothing. What's going on?"

"Nothing."

"Your phone is off. I looked for you at the cemetery."

I pulled at a blade of grass and chewed on it. "What do you need?"

"The last barista didn't show up this morning, so the coffee shop never opened."

"Bummer."

"Yeah," Britney said. "It sucks. I'm hoping you might come back for a little while, just until I sell it or we hire some more workers."

"Double the pay."

"What? You want to be paid double?"

"No," I said. "I don't want to be paid at all. But you should double the pay of workers. Offer them a bonus to stay a month, like a full month of pay."

"I'm not doing that."

I chewed more grass, rolled on my side, turning my face away from her.

"Okay, fine. I'll do it. But you have to help me train them so I can sell that damn place."

As Britney unlocked the coffee shop door and walked

in, two men in dress shirts walked in behind us. They seemed confused, but stepped up to the register when I walked behind the counter. They ordered coffee, and I took their money. I felt stupid.

While I prepared two pour-overs, Britney walked through the galley kitchen checking supplies or something, then stood next to me. "You'll be okay?"

"Sure."

"Bring me something to eat," I said. "From the vegan place."

She nodded. "Thanks again."

There was a steady stream of customers and I felt anxious, confused by why I'd agreed to help her. As the lunch-time rush grew, I stopped accepting money, which confused the customers.

"You can have the coffee," I repeated. "I don't want your money."

"Are you going out of business?" the man who asked for the coffee said.

"No."

"Then I should give you money."

The man behind him piped in, "Just take it. It's free."

"Then they'll go out of business," the first man said.

"That's their problem," the second man said.

"Hold on."

I went to the kitchen and wrote a note: "Pay what you want," which I taped to an empty cardboard box. I set the box at the end of the counter.

"Alright," the first man said. He left money in the box.

The second man ordered a latte but didn't leave

money. He didn't thank me, either.

But almost everyone else who came in left something. It was the first time I enjoyed making coffee drinks.

When Britney returned around eleven o'clock, she was more confused than the customers.

"What in the actual fuck are you doing?"

"Giving away coffee."

"But that's not a business," she said.

"It seems to work," I said. "I think there's more money in the box than we normally bring in."

"You're fucking insane."

I took the food she brought and sat at the table to eat. People came in and helped themselves to the brewed coffee, some of them leaving money in the box.

Britney sat beside me and ate a French fry from my lunch. "The minute I find someone to replace you, you're fired."

24

DAVID

DAVID VISITED WILKERSON & ASSOCIATES. THE BUILDING was in the office complex beside the Briarwood Mall, one of ten identical buildings with various company names displayed on the sign above the door. This building was also home to a financial advisor, a podiatrist, and a video production company.

David carried his briefcase into the office and pressed the button on the reception desk to notify them of his arrival. A man's voice from inside the office space called out, "Hang on."

As David waited, he realized he was wearing the same clothes since Friday, when the crisis first struck. Before he could check to see if he had body odor, the door opened.

A man in a business suit offered his hand. "Skyler Webber."

"David Rice."

Skyler Webber had cool, light-brown skin. His dark hair was cropped close, like he might be ex-military. He smiled slightly, nodded, and seemed at ease.

David relaxed as he followed Skyler into the office space. "Quiet around here."

"It's just me," Skyler said. "Wilkerson & Associates is a national firm, and I'm opening up this office. Once I drum up enough business, we'll staff up."

"So you're new to investigations?"

Skyler offered David a seat but remained standing on the other side of the desk. "I was a Michigan State Police Investigator for two decades. I worked for another private investigation firm the last two years when this opportunity came up."

"Sounds good."

Skyler sat down and smiled again. "How can I help you?"

David explained his business, their expanding revenue, and concerns about dropping profit over the past few years. "It's kind of embarrassing, but we use Excel spreadsheets to keep the books. I know we use QuickBooks, but the CFO uses spreadsheets to create all the financial statements."

Skyler nodded. "And?"

"I noticed a series of payments logged on the ledger sheet to a vendor I don't recognize. The transaction description says accounting services. When I looked for the vendor, I found nothing."

"They're a Michigan-based company?"

"An LLC, but when I checked the State's licensing system, the business is managed by a law firm. I was going to call around this morning, but realized I might tip someone off."

Skyler jotted down another note. "Do you have the

spreadsheets I can look at?"

David held up his briefcase. "Brought you a laptop."

"And is there an individual you suspect may be responsible for these payments?"

"Frank Marshall, our CFO. My wife recruited him and we've trusted him."

"I see."

"Maybe that's another thing I should be embarrassed about."

Skyler set down his pen. "Not at all. It's very difficult to suspect someone you trust. Also, access to money changes people, makes them skim a little, then a little more, then maybe a little more."

"The prick."

Skyler smiled again. "Or it could be a misunderstanding. We want to look at the data and be sure about what it is we're seeing."

David nodded. "You have the technical skills for this?"

"Computer forensics was my area. I'll bring in an associate for the accounting forensics. We'll track down the provenance of the business entities, see if we can attach names to anything, or make connections, and let you know."

"So I leave you with the laptop?"

Skyler reached a hand across the desk and turned it palm up. "We have the matter of payment."

"Money," David said. He handed the laptop to Skyler and took out his wallet. "Of course."

25

ASHLEY

I WAS AT THE COFFEE SHOP when my dad texted, "I'd like to speak with you."

I replied, "Call if u want".

"Where are you?"

"B's coffee shop".

"Okay," he texted. "I'll see you there in about twenty minutes."

It had been over a week since our incident at my house and the little matter of the cyber-attack on his company. I'd kind of been grateful for the work at the coffee shop, distracting myself from thinking about his betrayal, wondering about what I might do next, and ruminating about the felony I may have committed.

Also, I was still giving away the coffee, adding cold brew to the offering and lattes on demand. Donations had grown slightly day after day, and were profitable enough for Britney to put up with the experiment. Word had gotten around and the up-tick in customers was now obvious. There were busy times for working people, coming and going, and another at lunch for people grabbing a brew after eating.

Still not taking any pay, I read a book at a table until the coffee pots needed to be refilled or the donation box needed to be emptied.

This was a Monday morning, during the lull, when Britney walked in. She waved to me and checked the donation box, started a fresh pot of coffee, and sat next to me.

"I may have a buyer," she said. "At least they're interested."

"Good for you."

"I can't believe this works, giving away coffee, but this guy heard about it."

"He probably wants to franchise the idea," I said. "He'll make millions giving away coffee."

"Wait, do you think so?"

"No, but it's the right thing to do."

Britney glanced at her reflection on her phone's screen. "It's a stupid fucking idea and I can't believe I'm putting up with it."

"Found you a buyer."

"Probably a weirdo, like you."

"As long as his money's good, do you care if he's a weirdo?"

Britney picked away a tiny smidge of lipstick from a tooth. "Nope."

My father came in. He paused as if making an entrance, but it probably surprised him to see Britney. I wasn't sure why seeing Britney in Britney's coffee shop would surprise him, but I guessed he wanted to talk about something having to do with Sophie.

He sat at the next table. "Can we talk?"

"That's why you texted," I said.

"Can we talk privately?"

"You guys can talk," Britney said. She stood up. "I'll tidy up while I'm waiting for my weirdo. Besides, Ashley's not my employee."

Dad's face told me he didn't follow what she was saying, but I knew he would take yes for an answer.

"Let's step out," I said. "I probably should get some sunshine in case I'm thrown in the slammer next week."

We sat at one of the tables on the sidewalk. I chose a seat in the sunshine to warm up. My dad was restless, fidgeting, and looking around.

Four teenage boys walked into the coffee shop.

"The latte gang," I said.

My dad turned to me for an explanation.

"School's out. They come in every morning for lattes or whatever, because they're free."

"The boys are free?"

"The lattes are free."

"Since when?"

"Since I stopped charging for them."

He shook his head. "Okay…whatever…listen, I found out some things about the missing money. But, first, I'm sorry about what I said last week." He waited for my response.

I wasn't in the market for an apology. Besides, he mentioned the money before the apology. That's who he was: the money guy. So I waited.

"Okay?" he said. "I'm sorry, but you don't seem

impressed."

"What is it you're sorry about?"

"I'm sorry about how I treated you and that I wasn't sensitive to your feelings about your mother's death."

"And?"

"And what? That's it."

"Are you going to give the company to the employees and spend more time with me?"

He raised his hands like I was threatening him. "Is this why you're giving away coffee?"

One of the latte boys inside the coffee shop yelled, "But they're always free!"

"Not today," Britney shouted back.

Then all the boys shouted, their voices loud, a mix of baritone and girlish tenors, and Britney shouting for them to shut up.

My dad got up, and I followed him inside, where the shouting had quickly turned to pandemonium as one boy dragged the point-of-sale computer off the counter and kicked it, shattering the screen. Another boy hopped over the counter and threw coffee pots, racks of food—basically everything—to the floor.

Britney grabbed that boy but he shoved her away and Dad grabbed that boy and tried to drag him over the counter, but another boy swung a chair and knocked my father to the ground.

By then, the other boys were in the back room, pulling all the coffee beans to the floor. I cowered in the corner and watched as they flipped over tables and chairs.

A gun shot fired.

The boys hollered and screamed as they ran out of the store.

My father stood with his feet apart, bracing himself against the counter, and holding his small pistol by his side.

\# \# \# \#

BRITNEY SAT OUTSIDE THE COFFEE SHOP AND sobbed as an Ypsilanti police officer took her statement. I held her hand, offering napkins when she needed to blow her nose.

Her description of the incident was stilted, but it calmed her down. Eventually, she sounded like the over-achieving young woman who had gotten an MBA to go with her JD. I was confident she'd soon be in control of her emotions and focused, once again, on making money.

I don't think she'd be giving away coffee as a business practice ever again. But it was pretty clear to me that, had she given the latte boys free lattes, none of this would have happened.

The latte boys often threw money in the donation box. Not a lot, but it was something.

The police officer, a young man with a crew cut, thick arms, and wearing body armor with lots of gadgets in pockets, asked me about the boys.

"I don't know them."

"Do you know their names?"

I did not.

"Can you describe them?"

I put Britney's hand back in her lap. "Four teenage boys. Dark hair, sandy hair, almost blond hair…two of them have acne."

"You know nothing about them?"

"They like lattes."

The police officer checked his notes. "Who was it that gave away coffee for free?"

"I did. It was my idea."

"You didn't think people'd get mad when you stopped?"

"It wasn't my idea to stop."

Britney perked up. "Who the hell gives away seven-dollar lattes?"

"Seven sounds like a lot for a latte," the police officer said.

Britney clenched her fists in her lap. "Well then, get your coffee at McDonalds."

The police officer tapped his pencil on his notebook. "You going to be giving them away for free again?"

"No," Britney said.

They released my dad from the back seat of the police cruiser, where he'd been held for almost half an hour. It turned out he had a concealed weapon permit, but didn't have it on him. Just the gun, which was a little thing as far as guns go. It looked like a toy, to be honest, compared to what the cops had in their holster.

A police officer escorted Dad to his car, where he put the gun in the trunk. Then he joined us at the table outside the shop.

"Have you called Reuben?" Dad asked Britney.

"Who the hell is Reuben?" she asked.

"The insurance agent I set you up with."

"This will be covered?"

"It will be if you got the rioting rider." He looked up Reuben's phone number and showed it to Britney. "The rioting rider pays double indemnity, so this is probably a good thing. You can have the place gutted and it'll be easier to sell."

This cheered Britney up, and she went inside to place the call.

"Even now you only think of money?" I asked.

He opened his mouth to speak twice but stopped, fidgeted, and took a breath. "The other thing I wanted to tell you… Frank has been embezzling money."

"Easy come, easy go."

He chuckled, which I wasn't expecting. "It's made me think about what your mother wanted."

"You'll give the company away?" He flinched and waved my hands to quiet me down, but I was so surprised it just came out of me. "Sorry."

"No," he whispered. "What happened here today should tell you why. When you give people something for nothing, they don't respect it."

"You mean like how you gave Frank his salary for nothing and he stole money from you?" I whispered, but this still annoyed Dad.

He glanced inside the shop again. "That's different. That's an asshole taking stuff. But this—this was boys who felt entitled to those drinks even though they hadn't earned them — "

I shook my head.

"Fine. I don't want to argue about this, anyway. But I want you to know I'm going to move forward on the company thing because, well, I finally realize the company is not the same without your mother. It really hurt me that Frank stole. I thought we were like family, but I see we're not."

I think he wanted me to hug him or something, but his motivation was a bit off. I wasn't going to applaud him for planning a semi-convenient business decision that sort of fits with the promise he made to his wife on her deathbed. Still, it was a step in the right direction. "Good for you," I said. "I'll believe it when I see it."

"You can't breathe a word of this. I'm getting the evidence together, so it's going to get ugly."

A man with a camera approached and took a photo of the coffee shop. He wore a plain ball cap and dark sunglasses. He wore a windbreaker, which was a little weird because of the heat, but I didn't think anything of it. I didn't even think anything of him taking the picture. There had been gawkers across the street while the police were parked out front, and a few folks braved the activity for a closer look.

But my dad wanted to know why he took the photo. "Are you with the insurance company?"

"I'm a photojournalist," the man said.

"With which newspaper?" My dad sounded incensed. I chalked it up to his being overly-protective, and mostly I was glad his gun was in the trunk of his car.

The man turned his camera at us and snapped several photos. "Independent photojournalist," he said.

"Knock it off," Dad said. "Leave us alone."

184

26

DAVID

DAVID VISITED HIS LAWYER AND LONG-TIME friend, George Rohon, who had been the company's General Counsel at one point and was brought back to consult. But those consultations had dwindled the past few years as Jared was elevated to a pseudo-general counsel.

"Everything alright?" George asked. He was bald and had reddish-brown skin. He had kept a full beard in the past, but now he was sporting a trimmed goatee streaked with gray. "You haven't shown up unannounced since Heather passed away."

David's brow was furrowed, and he nodded briefly. "Got something to do, and I need your advice."

"I'm all ears." They sat in George's office in Plymouth, the upstairs suite of a building along the main street in the downtown district.

"First, I fired a weapon in a Depot Town coffee shop yesterday and they gave me a citation. I'll need you to go to court with me."

George stared. "Why in the world would you ever, ever discharge a weapon?"

David explained the recent events in a succinct but monotone delivery, showing it was just the appetizer.

"Holy shit," George said. "What's the main course?"

David explained the previous week's events, starting with the cyber-attack. "I was planning to call you to recommend a bankruptcy lawyer."

"But there was no ransom demand?"

"There's a demand for ransom, but it's emotional." He covered the situation with Ashley and Joan without mentioning that Ashley was Joan. There was only so much he could get into.

"That's quite a situation," George said. "So, what else is going on?"

"I looked at our accounts. Something I haven't done in a few years. I'd been entrusting Sophie to oversee the finances."

George inflated his lips as if he were about to make a rude noise, but let out a sigh. "What did you find when you looked at the accounts?"

"Frank has been skimming money, making payments to vendors that are owned by shell companies he controls. He's got a new house, a place up north, boats in Lake Michigan and Lake Erie, and some off-shore assets."

"Embezzlement?"

"Close to two million dollars."

George drummed his fingers on the desk, processing what he'd heard. "This was the guy that Sophie recruited?"

"That's the guy."

"Do you think Sophie knows?"

"No," David said. "I mean, she wouldn't just allow him to take money from us."

George nodded, rubbed the whiskers on his chin a few times.

"I mean, she's my wife, so the business is kind of hers, too."

"Is it?"

"Technically, I'm the only managing member of the LLC. But she, Frank, and a few other employees are members."

"Yes," George said. "I set that up for you."

"We have contracts for profit sharing," David said. "I generously compensate all the top managers."

"And yet…"

"And yet, here we are."

George fidgeted with a pen while thinking. "What is it you hope to do?"

"I want to bring charges against him and recover the money."

"You could have gone to the district attorney."

David ran a hand through his hair. "I'm not sure how Sophie will react."

"Mm-hmm."

"I don't believe she's cheating on me, if that's what that look implies."

George leaned his elbows on the desk. "That look was an I-told-you-so. I assume you've always wanted to leave the company for Ashley. If you'd gotten the prenuptial agreement, as I suggested, there wouldn't be anything to worry about."

David shook his head. "Ashley doesn't want the

company. She wants me to give it to the employees."

"Give it?"

"I don't want to do that," David said. "I'd sell it to them."

"Then what?"

"Then I'd spend more time with Ashley, I guess."

George patted the desktop with his hands. "I know Heather wanted that."

"Okay," David said. "Another great look from you. It wasn't so simple to just walk away from the company."

"I understand."

"I can't very well sell the company to anyone, especially the employees, with this mess hanging over it. And Sophie may protest, and who knows what after that."

George went to a cupboard at one end of the office and opened it to reveal a mini-bar. He poured two glasses of whisky.

"Hypothetically," George said, as he handed David a glass, "she could file for separation from the marriage and claim half the value of the business."

David sipped his drink. "She wouldn't."

"Or worse, she could insist on half ownership and managing it, using that to get you to pay her a premium to surrender the business."

"Ah crap," David said. "I hate talking to lawyers."

"I'm not even a divorce lawyer. You want to see some crazy shit, wait until you see the lawyers she can afford to hire. They are straight out of the bowels of hell."

"Okay, but we don't know for sure she's having an affair, or if she would stand in the way of a selling the company."

"But if she did, you'd have to leverage the business to pay her share, and then sell it."

"We hardly argue," David said. "There's nothing going on with her and Frank. Besides, it's my company to dispose of as I see fit."

George swirled his glass, sniffed the whisky, and drank. "And yet, your gut sent you here, rather than to the district attorney. You know it's a possibility."

David emptied his glass. "What are my options?"

George took their glasses back to the side cupboard. "Let's start with another drink."

27

ASHLEY

NOTHING FELT RIGHT. I HATED THAT I played a role in the violence at the coffee shop—even though I stood by my conviction that Britney triggered the actual riot. Britney was going to make money off of the insurance and had a clear path to gut the coffee shop and sell the building, which would make her more money and deprive the neighborhood of a pretty nice coffee shop.

I didn't even like that the latte boys made my father consider selling the business to the employees.

I'd gone home and tried to watch something to distract myself and ended up re-watching most of Sabrina the Teenage Witch, which I'd loved as a little kid. It was my go-to comfort television, but it didn't help.

I must have watched four episodes in a daze, staring at the screen but thinking about the empty feeling deep down in my stomach. The emptiness spread, sucking my lungs and my bowels into the void, hollowing me out. I felt my drool trickle down my chin and onto my upper chest. My eyes were dry and itchy from not blinking. My legs were numb, and I wasn't sure I could move them.

What was the point in trying to keep what was left of the family together when all they cared about was money?

Then I realized it was a despairing sense of doom that had taken hold of me. I had done a rash and illegal thing. I might be sent to jail, or at least alienate my father and Britney. How long before those wounds healed? What would we be like at that point?

I heard a cough outside and paused the TV. A twig snapped. I wanted to move, but it was like I'd forgotten how to command my body.

A car door opened and closed, and my heart raced. It was three o'clock in the morning.

I willed myself to get up. Peeking out the window, I saw a car at the curb I hadn't ever seen before.

This wasn't unusual. There were a lot of college-age kids who lived on the street and different cars came and went all the time. I'm something of a night owl, staying up late to read or watch TV, and I notice them. Rather, I make a note of them.

I'm not entirely comfortable living alone in a big house. It's generally safe, but no place is entirely safe, so I take precautions. I take notice.

Also, I don't use my phone for social media like other people my age. I have accounts everywhere, but I barely use them. Joan used to use them, but I wasn't interested. I'm more in tune to what's going on around me because of that, or so I like to think.

Again, it's probably the source of a lot of my anxiety.

Noticing things are different and wondering why. Instead of the anxiety brought upon by the artificial world of social media, I have the anxiety brought upon by the real world.

Sometimes I switch to a Joan mindset because Joan, although careful, does not worry as much as I do.

That's one thing I like about Joan.

I checked the doors (everything was locked) and lay down on my bed, staring at the ceiling until I eventually fell asleep as the first light of dawn emerged.

When I got out of bed two hours later, the mystery car was gone from where I'd seen it during the night. Despite my concern, hunger drove me out to forage for food and I walked down the street.

The mystery car was a few houses away and drove off as I approached. I didn't get a look at the driver.

As I walked back to my house with my vegan bagel with vegan cream cheese, I stayed vigilant, looking up and down the crossroads, glancing in driveways for the mystery car. There was no reason to worry, as no threat had been made or implied. It was merely a presence.

But worried I was.

Joan would not have worried, and that's part of what bothered me.

Joan would walk up to a car and ask the driver for a cigarette.

Joan would key the car and run away.

Joan would tell the driver to buy her a drink, then throw it in his face.

Joan would have forgotten about her father once it was clear he'd forgotten his promise.

Joan was a taker.

I wasn't Joan, though. I was Ashley, and Ashley hoped for her father to do the right thing ten years after his promise.

Ashley hoped to still have time with her father.

Ashley was a giver and a pleaser.

I wanted to be Ashley, but it was pretty clear that the world was full of Joans.

I visited my mother's grave that afternoon. It had gotten brutally hot, like a sweltering August day, but at the end of June, with swamp-ass humidity. It was later in the afternoon and the heat seemed to generate its own weather, the wind whipping around as clouds stacked up in the west and moved in.

In a far corner, someone drove a lawn mower up and down the rows. But I was the only visitor at the cemetery, unless you count the hawk sitting on a dead tree at the edge of the lawn. It focused its attention on the fields of tall grass to the south, where red-winged blackbirds, spaced evenly along the edge, chattered back and forth.

I stood before my mother and really had nothing to say to her. I let all my feelings of missing her fill my heart. I knew she loved me. I could feel that love pushing aside the loneliness.

Sweat beaded on my neck and along my hairline. I wore my Ashley wig, black jeans and a long-sleeve shirt.

The heat felt oppressive and more than a little sickening. Joan would have dressed in shorts and a tank top. She'd have a cute hat to block the sun.

Funny, but I wondered if my mother would recognize me dressed as Joan.

I needed a cool drink and to sit in the shade, but I wasn't ready to leave my mother just yet.

I recalled a classmate's birthday party in Ringerton. A piñata was strung up from the tree in the backyard. My mother was there to help, along with a few other moms. As the birthday girl swung blindly, my mother yelled, "Look out," a little too loudly. But she had been right: the blindfolded birthday girl smacked me in the head with the broomstick, knocking me to the ground.

A gust of humid air roused me from my memory. Overhead, a half dozen blackbirds mobbed the hawk, chasing it across the cemetery. As I followed their flight, I noticed a car parked at the other end of the cemetery. It was the mystery car. A man in a baseball cap and sunglasses stood on the far side of the car with a camera aimed at me.

It was a long way off, but I was sure it was the independent photo journalist from the coffee shop the day before. He got in the car and drove off.

I'd been warned. Someone was following me. The question was, who? The man who brazenly approached us at the coffee shop and followed me to the cemetery was almost certainly a private investigator. The next question was, who hired him?

Frank, who had been so incensed at Joan, popped into my mind.

28

I DROVE TO MY FATHER'S HOUSE IN Mansionville. As usual, I unlocked the front door with the electronic code and waited in the atrium, texting to let him know I was there.

Before he responded, Sophie appeared on the second story walkway. Her glasses were pushed back on top of her head and she held her phone with two hands. "Well, look who's here."

"Hello Sophie. I need to speak with my father."

"Good luck getting him to talk to you," she said. She glanced down at her phone and tapped on it, texting. "He's only come out of there for coffee and Pop Tarts the past two days. If you don't mind, tell him he has a wife that has a few things to say to him."

She turned and walked down the hall.

I started to take off my shoes but thought, fuck it. Maybe I don't want to.

My father didn't respond when I knocked on the door and for a moment I panicked, thinking he had died in there. I turned the knob, but the door was locked.

"Dad," I said. "Are you okay?"

"Yah," he called. He opened the door. "What's wrong?"

"Can I come in?"

"Of course."

With the door closed and me settled into the chair in the reading corner, I caught my breath. "Why are you barricaded in your office?"

"I really need to finish this thing, that's all." He typed something else, took a deep breath of his own. "What brings you here?"

"I'm being followed." I explained how I was pretty sure it was the guy who photographed us at Britney's coffee shop.

"That's not good."

"I don't know what to do."

"Maybe you should stay here a while."

I shook my head a little.

"You can have the entire wing, or you can stay above the carriage house."

I threw up a little at how he tossed off these terms so easily. Was this the vocabulary of a man who would sell his company to the employees at a discount? "Can you just let go of whatever it is you're doing, and let go of the company? Like now?"

"Now?"

"We could go live in the Ringerton house."

"I'm not going to just walk away from this."

I sat at the desk to be closer. "I need you, Dad. This has to do with whatever is going on with Frank. Let him have it."

He folded his hands on the desk. "It's a hell of a lot of money we're talking about. Crimes were committed."

"All the more reason."

"It's not right. I have to settle this before I can sell the company. I want everything in order."

I pulled my legs up and wrapped my arms around them. "He followed me to the cemetery. I don't want to feel unsafe visiting Mom."

Dad opened his desk drawer and took out his pistol, placing it next to his laptop.

I shook my head.

He reached in and took out a second one, identical to the first.

"No," I said.

"Honey, I'm not saying we're in danger, but it's better to be prepared."

"I hate guns. And why do you have two of them? That's insane."

"I got one for your mother."

"She carried it?"

He put one gun back in the drawer. "No. She didn't like them much."

"Then why'd you buy it?"

"I thought we should be ready to protect ourselves."

"Too bad you can't shoot cancer."

"You know what I mean. I think you should consider it."

"I'd be too afraid I'd shoot myself."

"We could get you some training," he said. "It'd be a father-daughter kind of thing."

"No."

He drummed his fingers on the pistol. "What about Joan?"

I glared. "What about her?"

"Maybe she'd consider it?"

29

DAVID

Dᴀᴠɪᴅ ʀᴇᴛᴜʀɴᴇᴅ ᴛᴏ ʜɪs ʟᴀᴡʏᴇʀ's ᴏꜰꜰɪᴄᴇ and said, "I know you called this meeting, but I have news."

George offered him coffee. As he handed over the mug, he said, "Do we need something stronger than this?"

"You first," David said.

"I spoke with the magistrate. The district attorney is not interested in pursuing the weapon discharge, given the circumstances and Michigan's Stand Your Ground law. Also, he knows you can afford more lawyer than just me."

"Is that it?"

"He'll want a misdemeanor charge for the weapon possession, given that you didn't have your concealed carry permit on you."

David nodded. "You don't want to fight it?"

"I think he's being generous."

"I can hire someone else."

George sipped his coffee. "Oh, you definitely need a defense attorney experienced with this judge and these charges."

David rattled his coffee mug on the desktop. "Can I keep my gun?"

"Are you expecting the four teenage boys to throw snowballs at your car?"

"Not in June."

"Yes, you can keep your gun." George leaned back in his chair. "It doesn't hurt that you're a major donor to the District Attorney's election campaign."

"That was done with sincere consideration."

"Mm-hmm."

"What?"

"Are we done here?" George asked.

David shook his head. "I have preliminary results from the forensic accounting investigation."

"Frank did what you think he did?"

"He did what I think. The private investigator tracked down Frank's financial statements and the shell companies he used to obscure it."

"That didn't take long."

"According to my guys, it wasn't terribly sophisticated."

"Ham-fisted?"

"No," David said. He leaned forward on the desk, his eyes wide open, his gaze steady. "They liked his approach, but it was only good enough to fool the IRS. The payments were to a local company that moved the money to an off-shore real-estate holding company. There's a loophole in IRS regulations about foreign companies purchasing property in America, and the off-shore company turned around and bought the house where Frank lives, plus a condominium near each of his boats, and another place on Torch Lake."

"Does your company own those properties, then?" George asked.

"No. They're deeded to the off-shore company. That company is owned by another shell company that lists a Delaware-based law firm as the contact. But the private investigator has proof Frank is the managing member."

George rubbed his thumb against his fingertips, as if preparing to count money. "Sounds like an expensive mess to unwind, regardless."

David sat back in his chair and sighed.

"Will you press charges?"

"I'm going to give him one chance to make it all right, give back the money, with interest, transfer the properties, whatever. I'll have the lawsuits ready to drop, and the info ready to give to the district attorney. Which is where you come in."

"Are you going to get my legal fees from him?" George asked. "I'm thinking this might get expensive."

JOAN

I KNOW YOU KNOW IT'S NOT me, but this is my story and my choice. These are my problems to solve.

I didn't know how to solve the problem of Frank's obsession with me. The thing is, you can't really solve it when someone becomes obsessed. You deal with it, turn it aside, move past it. Yes, I knew it was some kind of cheap ass private detective tailing me, but what would Frank do with that information?

Ashley could only passively deal with it, hiding behind locked doors, watching television until the world changed.

I attracted such a man at community college and when I told him no, he became incensed. It was scary. He yelled at me a few times, called me a slut and a whore. I got lucky that time.

Frank was too old for that, but he had the money to get what he wanted. His boy was stalking Ashley to get to me. So I was going to have to do something.

I dialed the number Frank wrote on the back of his business card.

He answered, saying, "Who is this?"

"Joan."

"Oh? You must know we guessed the goddam password. So what in the hell do you want?"

"I was going to ask you the same thing."

"What the hell is this?"

"There's a private investigator bothering my friend. I guess you're looking for me, but wanted to be sure."

There was noise in the background. Frank said something inaudible, then came back on the phone line. "How about we meet? I'll make it worth your while."

"I'll call you in thirty."

I hung up and removed the battery from the phone, a burner I'd purchased for the occasion, using cash, as one does, at a party store on West Michigan in Midtown. A girl can't be too careful.

I headed towards Ann Arbor.

I took precautions leaving the house, wary of the private investigator following Ashley. He'd gone missing after the cemetery, but we couldn't be entirely sure. I circled blocks, pulled into and out of parking lots, checking that no one followed me.

I had come up with a routine of leaving my car at a garage in downtown Ypsilanti. Ashley would drive the crappy Civic there, change clothes in the back seat, then get into "Joan's" Dodge Charger. It was our little superhero costume change moment.

The transformation was simple enough: Ashley wore a black, unruly, forgettable wig. I cut my natural hair short and dyed bright red. Remove the eyeglasses (which were clear lenses, anyway) and peel off the frumpy top. Slide into some skin-tight outfit and there was Joan. Pick out a pair of shoes from the trunk of the car and go.

I headed towards Frank's compound, which was off Huron River Drive, on the way to Dexter, past the pond where David and Sophie built their mansion. The sun was setting as I drove along the river, the turns putting the sun in my eyes over and over as the road twisted back and forth. When I arrived, darkness had fallen.

It reminded me of a time I went on a road trip, taking Route 12 west. Boring Ashley would never want to leave the area, but Joan wanted a pointless adventure. In Chicago, I found a place to eat with live music, drank wine that older men bought for me, the men not realizing—nor caring—that I was underage. I gave one guy a hand job in the back seat of his car, removed his hand from my left tittie, and drove back to Ypsilanti.

That's what this brief road trip on Huron River Drive felt like: getting a hand off my tittie.

I drove past Frank's house and parked the Charger up the street. Suddenly feeling conspicuous with my hair and my nipples showing through my top, I grabbed a ball cap and windbreaker out of the trunk of the car.

There was a steel gate in Frank's driveway with cameras trained on the apron. A stone wall stretched forty feet in both directions. It was all for show, though, as the stone wall receded into the ground and gave way to some shrubbery. There was no more fencing.

When the street was quiet, and well out of the view of the cameras at the driveway, I stepped through the shrubs and into his yard.

I powered up the burner and tried to figure out what I was going to do. My plan was to distract Frank and make him think Joan was out there, one step ahead of him, and mess with him. Keep his attention on Joan while David did his thing.

The house was on a one-acre lot, same as all the

houses on this stretch of road. There were trees along both the sides, with an enormous lawn out front. In the partial light, I saw into the backyard where the lawn sloped down to the river.

I was confident that no one could see me among the trees between the houses. They carved these lots out of woods.

I dialed Frank's special number again. "I'd like to meet?" I asked.

"What do you want?"

"Money."

Frank snickered. "You want a job?"

"If that's what it takes."

"Interesting."

"Why did you want to meet?" I asked again. I heard a door close and what sounded like Frank dropping his bulk into an office chair.

"I'm always looking for talent. You seem pretty good at what you do, albeit illegal."

"I did nothing illegal."

"Okay, well, I'm not interested in that," he said. "I admit I have a thing for redheads."

"What sort of thing?"

He snickered. "Come on. I know your type."

I mulled over my response. "How much?"

"A thousand dollars. All I want to do is get a good look at you."

"Cash?"

"Of course."

"Your place?"

"No. Don't be stupid."

"Nice," I said. "I'll meet you at the Blind Pig."

"That's even dumber."

"Meet me at the Blind Pig and we'll see how it goes." I hung up.

About three minutes later, the garage door opened, and a Porsche backed out, turned around on the tarmac, and drove down the driveway.

The back door to the walkout basement was open. Inside was an immense room like an upscale tavern with a bar at one end, a pool table, dining tables with chairs, and a sofa positioned in front of a ginormous television.

It wasn't all that different from the lower level in David and Sophie's mansion.

I went upstairs hoping to find his home office. I walked down the back hall but there was a laundry and a walk-in pantry, stocked for the apocalypse or something. At the end of a hall was a door to the garage and a staircase—the back staircase—up.

My plan was to infect his home PC with ransomware again. It was a version from the kit I'd used to infect the business, but with all the options selected. It would let me spy on him first, record his keystrokes, and send his passwords to a server on the dark web. It would likely ruin him.

I'm not saying it was a good plan. But Ashley was being tormented, and it compelled Joan to do something about it.

The top floor was a long hallway of rooms with no open atrium like in other fancy houses. The first four rooms were unoccupied, one empty, two of them with furniture, the last one a bathroom big enough for a dining table.

On the other side of the main staircase, there were two furnished bedrooms and two more bathrooms. At the end were two more doors. One was probably the master, the other an office.

I picked door number one. When I flipped on the light, I saw it was the main bedroom. Someone in the bed stirred and sat up.

That person was a woman—Nikki, the controller from the company—who saw me, shouted, and fell out of bed.

I hurried down the hall for the stairs. As I made the first turn, she was behind me at the top of the stairs— Christ, she was fast for a pregnant woman. She was wearing a T-shirt and sweatpants, and holding a gun in her hands pointed at my face.

DAVID

DAVID FELT DRAWN TO VISIT HEATHER'S grave. The cemetery, being older, didn't have gates or lighted paths. Beyond the tall grass outside the fence, the lights of Ringerton shone across the water. He drove in the darkness to the far corner and parked, leaving the headlights on. Seeing no other cars, he assumed he was alone among the headstones.

As he walked up to Heather's grave, David felt another presence. He paused and looked around, but no one was there.

The car's headlights cast David's shadow across the lawn to the edge of the cemetery. It only took a minute to find Heather's marker. As he stood over it, he grew agitated. Something bothered him.

The problems with Frank, the embezzlement, and Ashley's insistence that he sell the company made him want to drink and forget it all. Sophie had been pestering him for days and he knew better than to share anything with her. He'd hoped visiting his wife's grave would bring comfort. Or something. He wasn't exactly sure why he was there.

Ashley's words sounded in his mind: *She'll help with this decision.*

"I miss talking to you about the business," he said. The words surprised him. Strangely worried he might have insulted his deceased wife, he added, "And other things, of course. I just miss you."

"Look," he heard Heather say. It was in his mind,

but the voice was distinct.

At the edge of the cemetery, in a gap in the fence, two green orbs—a pair of eyes—glowed. Then two more glowing eyes beside the first two.

A moment later, three more sets of eyes joined the first pair. They moved toward him and into the light.

Coyotes.

David backed away from the grave, then turned and hurried to the car. He didn't look back until the car door was closed with him safely inside.

The pack of coyote stood watching. When he started the car, they turned and ran back into the brush.

David called Ashley as he drove out of the cemetery. It rang six times, but she didn't pick up. He was overwhelmed with dread and dialed her number again.

JOAN

"WHAT DO YOU WANT?" NIKKI SHOUTED. The handgun wavered, but was still pointed at my face.

I showed her my palms and shook my head, my heart pounding in my chest. "I was looking for Frank."

"He would have shot you." Her T-shirt stretched across her pregnant belly as she shifted her grip on the handgun.

"I just wanted to talk to Frank. I'm sorry I disturbed you. I know you need your sleep—"

"Shut up."

I took a breath. "I know you won't shoot me because I can see the safety is on."

Nikki blinked, turned the gun slightly as she glanced at it, and I took off down the stairs.

She squeezed off a round, and I screamed, but I made it to the front door and got out, struggling with the lock for half a second—which seemed an eternity—and sprinting into the darkness.

I ran straight for the trees beyond the decorative lawn lighting and weaved through the trees toward the neighbor's lawn.

She fired two more shots. I don't know if they were close, or if she even knew where I was at that point, but each blast made me gasp and run a little faster. Also, I peed my pants.

DAVID

DAVID DROVE TO ASHLEY'S HOUSE. THE driveway was empty, the garage door closed, and the house was dark. He hoped that Ashley had simply turned in for the night.

As he cut the engine and got out of the car, a figure—a young man—emerged from behind the house and stood in the driveway, bathed in the car's headlights. David's hand slipped into his jacket pocket, but he realized both of his guns were back at the home office.

"Oh hey," the young man said as he approached.

"Jared?" David called out. "What're you doing?"

"Looking for Joan."

"But why are you here?"

Jared waved toward the house. "I thought Ashley might know where she is."

"Doesn't look like she's home," David said. "So maybe call it a night."

Jared offered a closed-lip smile. "Joan broke into Frank's house tonight. The police are investigating."

David nodded as he studied Jared's face, half of it cast in shadow. He was clean-shaven, his hair styled and falling to one side, cropped short above the ears. He wore a silk shirt, chinos, and loafers. "Stay away from Ashley. You got a problem with Joan, take it up with Joan."

Jared patted David's shoulder. "This is serious. I know you know because Joan almost ruined us, but this is some weird, scary stuff going on. We don't want anyone to get hurt."

"Stay away from Ashley," David said. "Understand?"

"Of course," Jared said. "Maybe you don't see it because she's Ashley's friend, but this Joan is strange. I'm trying to help."

"That's enough," David said.

"Call Frank and see if you can assure him because he's pretty upset with Joan."

The car's headlights turned off, darkness falling as his eyes adjusted. Jared lingered, but David said no more.

He waited until Jared drove away and turned the corner. He lingered out front to be sure Jared wasn't doubling back.

30

ASHLEY

AFTER MAKING THE SWITCH IN THE Ann Arbor parking garage, I drove straight to Mansionville. As much as I hated the house that Sophie built, I didn't want to go alone to my dark place in Depot Town. Staring at a gun scared Joan to death, and I didn't know what to do with that.

I entered the pass code for the front door but it didn't open. I knocked on the door and peered through the sidelight.

Sophie emerged from the hallway to my father's office. Reluctantly, she made her way downstairs and let me in.

"When did you change the code?"

"Just this morning," she said. "I'm sure you understand."

I expected her to tell me the new code, but she stared, her eyebrows raised slightly, her mouth in a polite smile.

"I need to see my dad."

"He's not at home," she said. "I suggest you call. Tell

him I said hello. He's been distant lately. Distracted."

I smiled politely. "I'm sure it's nothing."

As I fumbled with my phone, Sophie said, "Did you hear the news? Joan broke into Frank's house. Strangest thing. Almost got herself killed."

I stopped dialing mid-number. My heart raced, and I felt the heat rush up my neck and into my face. From this distance, I couldn't be sure about what I saw in Sophie's face, whether she was mad at me or just mad at the world. "Is Joan okay?"

"She ran off into the night." Sophie folded her arms, tucking the phone with one hand while tapping an incisor with the manicured nail on the other. "Bizarre, really. Frank's upset, as you can imagine."

"Of course."

"Do you know where Joan is?"

My throat tightened, and I croaked, covering it with a cough. I felt sick, like I might vomit. Once I'd made it back to my car safely, and realized I hadn't been shot, I was relieved. Then I started shaking from the adrenaline. But I hadn't thought about how other people would be involved.

"Are you okay?" Sophie asked.

"I choked on my saliva."

Sophie scowled like I was a dog who pissed on her carpet. She pulled her eyeglasses from the top of her head and settled them on her nose, scrutinizing me for a moment. "Try reaching out to Joan again. The police are involved, of course. It would mean a lot to me if you could help. I don't want this upsetting your father anymore than it has already."

"I'll try."

"Thank you darling," she said. "Are you hungry? We have salads and something in there you can probably eat. You look famished."

I shook my head. "I'm going to call him from his office, if that's okay."

"I'm sure that's what he would want."

"I'll try Joan, as well."

"Tell her we care about her," Sophie said. "She needs help, and that's all we want for her."

DAVID

David had never warmed to Jared, and now he hated him. No telling what a moron who always thinks he's right might do, especially when they were raised by a family with enough money to fix anything the moron fucks up.

Jared had been a problem in high school—or so he'd heard from Sophie. The problems amplified in college. Still, they had enough money to get him into law school.

Jared was a competent lawyer, but it was still a stretch to use him as their General Counsel. Sophie had framed it as a favor to Frank, who was an asset to the company (her words) and Jared would come at a bargain. David trusted her. Given what he'd learned this past week, it wouldn't be a surprise to find out Jared took home more salary than everybody, except Frank, of course.

Finally convinced that Jared wasn't lurking around the corner, David approached Ashley's house and knocked on the door. He felt foolish for not being the type of father who was trusted with a key to his daughter's house.

He felt foolish that his relationship with Ashley had deteriorated to the point of her inventing a false identity to make a point. How could he stand there and criticize Jared's parents when he had created this situation with Ashley?

"Ashley?" he called out, but not so loud as to arouse

the neighbors. He felt a fool being that guy outside, on the porch at night.

He felt doubly foolish for not simply calling her, and he dug his phone out of his pocket.

ASHLEY

I LOCKED MYSELF IN MY DAD'S office. That calmed me and I sat in his reading chair with my legs pulled up and my arms wrapped around them.

My dad called before I was ready to dial his number. He sounded as relieved to hear my voice as I was to hear his.

"Stay in my office," he said. "Everything's going to be fine. Wait until I get there."

"How long?"

"However long it takes to drive from your house."

After a couple of minutes, it occurred to me that Joan would not sit around and wait. Joan had gotten into a shootout; also, Joan survived the shootout.

I'd risked my life, but learned a bit about who I was dealing with. These people—Sophie, Frank and Nikki— were absolutely focused on themselves.

Out of morbid curiosity, I checked the drawer where Dad kept those guns. It was unlocked.

I pulled the gun box out of the drawer. I took a breath and peeked inside: it was empty, which meant he had both guns with him.

As tonight showed, neither I nor Joan like guns. I worried about Dad out there with a gun, thinking he was safe because of it. Nikki had fired three rounds into the darkness. Would Dad be quick enough on the draw if it came to that?

I became sick to my stomach again. What if Nikki had killed me? Would anyone know I wanted to be buried next to my mother?

How did Sophie know about the shooting already? What if Frank somehow figured out that I was Joan, and was lying in wait to ambush my dad?

I had to get up and touch the books on the shelf to calm down. I found one I knew my mother had read — *a* — and held it close. She had once touched these pages. After I read it I cried at the ending but also because I knew I couldn't talk to my mother about the story. I realized that if I died, I might talk to her about the book. Oddly, that made me want to see my dad, and make up with him, because I didn't want us to keep arguing.

I wanted to ask my dad if he read that book. I wanted to read some book my father had read and then talk to him about it.

I wanted us to live a life that was so boring and uncomplicated that there was no reason to have guns. I wanted to live in a place that was so unremarkable no one would think of keeping a gun to defend it. I wanted to live with neighbors who helped each other, and no one worried about being robbed or attacked.

Maybe that's a lot to ask. But if there's one thing I learned from Joan, if you don't ask, you never get.

# # # #

My mother was a petite blond. She lost her hair to the chemotherapy, and I thought that was it: losing her hair was the bad thing that happened. I was an ignorant kid and didn't know what death meant.

The cancer went into remission, and it was a joyous time. Dad went back to being his old self, working and playing, and Mom was quieter than before but happy. Her hair grew back curly with streaks of auburn.

I stumbled on some web pages and figured out how bad cancer was, and that death was kind of forever, at least in our earthly state of being. When the cancer came back, I was worried, prone to anxiety attacks, and hyper-sensitive to anything about my mom. Like if she coughed or sneezed, I wanted her to call her doctor.

My worry became almost a joke. Then one morning, she coughed up blood.

My grandparents on Mom's side picked me up from school that day because Mom and Dad were at the doctor.

Mom was so sick that they didn't bother with chemo. She had some radiation treatments which I thought were a way to make her better, but it turned out it was to slow down the cancer and give her a few more weeks with us.

We set up hospice care in the house, turning the front room into Mom's room. Even though I had learned about death, I hadn't experienced it yet, at least not with someone I loved, and didn't know what to expect.

"I'll miss you," I told her one day, and cried.

Mom pulled me close and stroked my hair. "I'll stay with you in your heart."

"But what if I have to ask you something?"

"Ask me," she said. "Listen carefully for my answer."

"You promise?"

She smiled. "I can't promise that. I don't know what it's really like, but I know you'll feel my love all of your life, and that's what matters most. My answer will be in the love you feel."

I didn't really like that answer, but it seemed to make sense in the moment. I mean, I didn't expect to actually hear her.

The day before she died, she lay in complete stillness on the bed and I thought she was dead.

"Mom," I shouted.

She opened her eyes and smiled. Her hair spread across the pillow. Her blue eyes glistened with tears. Her lips were pale but glowed in the moment as she smiled. She looked like an angel.

My mother had been an angel. As an engineer, she helped develop the product to remove toxic, industrial sludge from contaminated lakes. When the business they created started making serious money, she refused to buy fancy clothes, cars, or a bigger house. The extra money went to charities or community projects. She talked my father into sharing profits with the employees.

My father rushed into the room. "What's going on?"

Mom took his hand. "Give the company to the employees and spend more time with Ashley. Don't let the business consume you."

Dad nodded.

"I mean it David," she said. "I won't be there to pull

you back into the family. Sell the company to the employees if you must, but give them a hell of a deal. Promise me."

"I promise," he said.

"Say it."

"I'll sell the company to the employees. I'll give them a hell of a deal. I'll spend my time with Ashley."

"Thank you."

I held Mom's other hand, and she squeezed it. We cried. It was sad as fuck. But I felt good knowing my father wouldn't get sucked into the company, going wild making all kinds of money.

I stayed home from school the next day and we were holding her hands again when she died.

DAVID

THE DOOR CODE DIDN'T WORK AND David had to find his key to unlock the door.

"Sophie?" he called.

"That's you, David?" she called from the upper landing.

Flustered, David dropped his keys. "What's the big idea?"

"I had to change the code," she said.

"Why?"

"I just had to."

"That makes no sense."

"You've been very distant lately," she said. "I don't know what's going on with you."

David set down his briefcase to cross his arms. "What in the actual fuck is wrong?"

"You should tell me what the actual fuck is wrong, darling. You've hardly said a word the past week, there are clandestine meetings at all hours, and you go everywhere with that briefcase all but handcuffed to your wrist. So is it someone else, or is there a drug habit I need to know about? Perhaps you're selling state secrets to the Iranians?"

"I'm working on a business problem."

"Wonderful," Sophie said. "As your business partner, I'd think you'd confide in me."

"I need to work it out for myself."

"Of course. Meanwhile, someone broke into Frank's house earlier. You're up to something, and I need to be informed."

David heaved a sigh and stared at the floor.

He married this woman for a reason, but at the moment he couldn't recall what it was. She'd understand once he explained, but he wasn't ready yet. Years of disagreement taught him to broach subjects only when his position was certain. She could turn anything into a fight, played the hurt feelings card like a pro, and brooded for weeks if necessary.

She was forcing him to decide early.

"Let me go talk to Ashley. Then I'll come up to your room."

"Fine. I'll go reset the alarm."

"What's the password?" David shouted after her.

"I'll tell you after you speak with your daughter, as that's clearly the most important thing in the world to you right now."

31

ASHLEY

My dad came into the office and pressed his ear to the door after he closed it, holding up a hand to shush me.

"What?" I whispered.

Satisfied, he gently locked the door. He turned on a Bose speaker playing white noise and turned up the volume. Finally, he set his briefcase on the coffee table and motioned for me to join him on the sofa.

"I'm a little worried about a couple of things with Sophie and Frank," he whispered. "I think there's something going on."

"That sucks," I said. "I'm sorry, I guess."

Dad nodded absently, thinking. I knew he knew I hated Sophie. I think he knew Sophie hated me, although he didn't always know it. He was oblivious to everything but her and the business for quite a while.

"What the hell were you doing at Frank's?" he asked. "That was you, right? There's not someone else who looks like Joan? Or is there an actual Joan?"

"It was me," I whispered.

"Okay. Well?"

"I'm not sure what I was thinking. I felt I had to do something to Frank and Joan is good at doing things."

"Tell me everything that happened."

I told him the first part of what I had done, how I lured Frank out and went in the back door, made a crack about Frank's home security being as lax as the security he implemented at the company—my dad wasn't in the mood to appreciate that—and how I was going to infect his laptop at home.

He sat back on the sofa and groaned. "I told you I was working on this. I'm trying to do what you want me to do."

"It's not what I want. It's what Mom wanted. If you're doing it for me, it won't work. You're missing the point."

"Okay," he said. "You're right. I'm sorry. I've come around to it."

"What does that mean?"

He smiled a little. "Seeing what Frank was doing to me, and what I think Sophie has done, it made me realize you're right. Your mother was right. I need to be done with the business. It'll be good for me."

"Oh."

"Yeah."

"That's good."

"Yeah. We've got enough money. It's going to be fine."

"There's one more thing about Frank's house."

He cocked his head and raised his eyebrows. I told him about Nikki and the gun, how she fired two or three rounds at me as I ran away.

"Holy shit."

"Yeah."

"I'm so sorry, honey."

"I shouldn't have been there. Joan was kind of stupid."

He checked the door and paced a bit. When he sat on the sofa again, he told me about Jared lurking at my house. "Maybe Jared's got a thing for Nikki."

"Is Frank the father of her baby? Or is it Jared?"

My dad thought a moment, baffled. "I assumed she had a boyfriend. I really don't know."

"So, what're you going to do?"

"Fire Frank." He whispered so softly I barely understood him over the white noise machine. "Demand the money back. Start legal proceedings."

"And?"

"Tell Sophie I'm selling the company to the employees. She'll be upset, but I'll have to buy her off."

"Okay."

"Yeah. It's going to be okay. I'm done." He seemed relieved. Hearing himself say it released tension from his face.

"I'm proud of you, Dad."

"Thanks, Sweetheart."

He grabbed his briefcase and rummaged through his desk, tossing more things into the briefcase, grabbing files from the credenza. He got a leather weekender from the closet and handed it to me.

"Pack the photo albums and any books you want," he said.

"Why?"

"I'm going to tell Sophie first, and it might be a little weird around here. We'll get a couple of rooms at the hotel—no, we'll go to George's and stay there. That way we can get started on the legal filings, and I'll call the security team, maybe even head over to the office tonight, still, and you can stay with George."

He had that slightly detached look I'd seen in him hundreds of times when he's working out something complicated, his brain generating options, pruning the low-value branches, trying to zero in on the best path. He tried to explain it to me once how he looks for a certain threshold value with minimal risk and shortest time to complete. Not the best option, but a good enough choice for the time available to evaluate. I think it always broke his heart a little that my brain didn't work like a really smart computer expert programmed it. Eventually, he realized few people could think like he did—Mom was maybe the only person who could do it better—and so he just did it and told his team what to do, rather than trying to get them to think like he did.

"What do you think Sophie's going to do?"

"Scream at me," he said. He smiled, which I hadn't expected. "She won't like any of this."

"So you're leaving her?"

I whispered it so softly that he had to think a moment to figure out what I asked. "Maybe. We'll see."

I motioned to the weekender bag.

"I'll tell her I'm taking you home, that you're upset, and I'll be back later to continue the discussion. But once we go, I won't come back. At least not tonight."

I was hopeful. It seemed I would get that chance to

spend time with him. I could ask him what his favorite book was, and then I could read it, and we could talk about it.

"Are you sure you're ready for this?" I asked.

He checked his watch. "At this hour, she'll have started drinking…" He went to the closet and pulled out two shirts and handed them to me. "She'll throw her drink in my face—won't be the first time—so I'll need to change later on."

"Jeez, Dad…"

"But I absolutely won't tell her I'm leaving because she'll claim abandonment of property and I'm not giving her everything just like that."

I raised my hands.

He smiled again and went to the bookcases, pulling out albums and books. When he stacked about a dozen on the corner of the desk, he took a breath and waggled his head to loosen his neck.

"It's going to be fine," he said. "Pack these and whatever else. Keep your shoes on and we'll head out in a few minutes."

He turned off the white noise machine, hugged me, and left the office.

I locked the door and packed the bag. I grabbed some books, found another photo album he missed, and packed all the photos with me or Mom. None with Sophie, obviously.

It'd been a few minutes, and I was ready. I pressed my ear to the door, expecting to hear shouting or at least raised voices. Sophie was likely in her office, which was upstairs. Still, if he'd left the door open—and there was no reason for him to close it—I'd certainly hear a loud conversation.

Instead, I heard a single gunshot followed by the dull thud of a body collapsing to the floor.

32

DAVID

As David lay on the floor, feeling woozy, and distantly aware that he was bleeding, he remembered a summer day in his Dearborn neighborhood. He was twelve and one of many latch-key kids on the street. His close friends and classmates lived across town, far enough away that he had to make an effort to meet them, so he was mostly on his own during the summer. There were high school-age boys in the neighborhood, but they didn't include him in their shenanigans.

He didn't mind. He spent mornings in the basement learning to program the Commodore 64 he'd gotten for his birthday. When David emerged from the basement this day, the sun beat down from a cloudless sky. He squinted at the light pouring into the kitchen windows.

After two bowls of Lucky Charms, he went out back.

David's father had tools, engines, and broken electronics in the garage, things he repaired in his spare time for cash. David spent afternoons taking those things apart and putting them back together, sometimes fixing things, but usually making them worse. He started a fire in the garage once and was careful not to do it again.

He kept the garage door up and the lone window open to allow a breeze, but the heat had already built up and gotten worse.

After an hour, feeling sleepy, or maybe feeling faint, he staggered out of the garage and used the hose to get a drink and douse his head.

"You okay?" Gretchen, the girl who lived next door, asked.

"Trying to cool off."

Gretchen was barefoot. She wore a pool wrap and carried a towel and a can of Diet Coke. She was sixteen. There was an above-ground pool in the backyard where Gretchen spent most afternoons on a float in the water listening to WRIF.

"You want to take a swim?" she asked.

He ran inside to put on trunks. He stripped off his jeans but hesitated because the trunks were hand-me-downs from his cousin Peanuts, and there was a tear in the waistband. He had vowed to never wear the hideous, brown paisley trunks when his mother presented them, but he had no way to get to the city pool, anyway, so it was mostly the theater of the young and powerless. Grateful they hadn't been thrown away, he put them on and went next door.

He turned the corner of the garage and froze: Gretchen's friend Lori was there, rubbing lotion on Gretchen's shoulders. He took a step closer, then another.

"Who's that?" Lori asked.

"David from next door."

"What's he doing here?"

"He's going to swim."

Gretchen waved him closer, pointed at the pool, and whispered something to Lori. David obeyed, climbed the ladder, and jumped in, the shock of cold hitting his bones.

David watched from below the surface as Gretchen jumped in, her body coated in air bubbles for a few amazing seconds until her dog-paddling shook them loose.

He surfaced for a breath, and Gretchen splashed him in the face. "How d'you like it?"

He nodded, afraid to smile and give away his joy in the moment.

ASHLEY

I WAS IN SOPHIE'S OFFICE AND threw myself to the floor where my father was coughing blood. I looked up at Sophie for help but she stared, the gun in her hand by her side.

"What did you do?" I screamed.

"It just happened," she said and walked out.

I called 911 and screamed about Dad, the dispatcher telling me to, "Calm down," over and over.

He coughed blood into my face and, oddly, I calmed down. Something about tasting my father's blood put me on a different plane of existence. There was him and me; nothing else mattered.

His eyelids fluttered, and I saw his eyes move and look directly at me. It was for half a second, but I know he was with me. He gurgled blood, and I realized he was choking. I pulled him onto his side and blood gushed out of his mouth. I leaned down and heard him take a breath.

I got back on the phone and explained how my dad needed an ambulance and I gave the address, described the house.

"What happened?" the dispatcher asked.

"He's been shot."

"Where?"

I checked his shirt, then noticed a wound under his chin. "The mouth, into his head."

"Is he breathing?"

"Yes, but he's still bleeding."

"Can you apply pressure to the wound?"

I grabbed a handful of tissues from the box on the desk, wadded them up, and shoved them into his mouth, pressing with my finger until I found the bullet hole.

"Keep talking to him," the operator said. "Tell him to stay with you."

Sophie came to the doorway a few times. I was pressing tissues into the wound, sobbing as I stroked my dad's head.

Sophie just stood there a moment before leaving again.

At some point, I heard her say, "Oh, thank God."

"Is it the ambulance?" I shouted.

She was on the upper landing, and she started down the stairs, her heels beating out unhurried steps. A moment later, heavy steps hurried up the stairs.

A short man wearing a suit leaned into the room, clutching the door frame to support himself. "He's alive?"

"Yes."

"Good."

"Who the fuck are you?"

"I represent Ms. Rice."

It confused me until I realized it was her goddam lawyer. Before I could scream, Sophie shouted that the ambulance had arrived.

Police stormed up the stairs with guns drawn and stepped into the room. "Where's the gun?" one of them shouted.

"Ask Sophie."

When the paramedics came into the room, one police officer escorted me down to the kitchen.

He was gentle, I suppose, but there was a lot going on. He kept asking what happened. I kept asking about my father.

I told him what I knew, that I'd heard a shot, ran to the room, and saw Sophie standing with the gun.

I was remarkably calm, but that was probably because the medics were with Dad. They carried him down the stairs, so I got up to follow, but the officer told me to sit back down.

"I have to go with him."

"Not yet."

I became hysterical, and another cop helped restrain me, at which point I sobbed uncontrollably.

I was certain they were going to arrest me, but Britney showed up and talked with the officers, working it out so I could leave.

Britney drove me to the hospital and guided me inside. I flinched and froze just inside the doors. The lights and smells brought back a flood of terrible memories of visiting my mother. I had that out-of-body, surreal feeling of knowing I'm in a place I don't want to be but also thinking it's not possible to be there, so I must be asleep, and the nightmare will be over if I wake up.

But I couldn't wake up.

Britney talked to the staff, got me a wheelchair and a set of scrubs to replace my blood-soaked clothing. She wheeled me to the restroom and helped me clean up and change clothes.

When we got to the nurse's station, they told us that Dad was in surgery.

Britney wheeled me to a visitors' lounge and got me arranged on something like a sofa. She sat tight up against me.

At some point, my glasses fell off. Britney wiped them clean and realized there was no prescription. "They're just for show?"

She put them on my face and said nothing else about it. We sat together in the visitor area all night.

DAVID

HE FELL IN LOVE WITH HEATHER the moment he saw her. It was the first week of classes and she was across Palmer field, among the hundreds of students who came outside in the evening to enjoy the sunlight and warm weather of early September. She'd been playing touch football wearing jeans and a yellow, button-down oxford, the only woman dressed like that.

Her shoulder-length hair caught his eye. Her smile, exuberant and contagious even from two hundred feet away, kept his attention. When she and her friends went back into Alice Lloyd, he was crushed because his room was in Couzens Hall.

He glimpsed her once or twice a week, coming or going to classes, and he dragged his roommate to any rumored parties at Alice Lloyd, but it wasn't until second semester when they were both in Mechanics—the only freshmen in that class—that they finally met.

Then he was trapped in a laboratory, maybe on campus, maybe somewhere else, and equipment ran all around him, chirping and counting and measuring.

He wanted to talk to Heather about it. She'd know what to do. He knew with absolute certainty that, for any problem, she'd always known what to do.

But he didn't know where she was.

33

ASHLEY

GEORGE AND HIS WIFE, MICHELLE, TOOK me to their home, where I collapsed on the couch. I woke up with my shoes pulled off and a blanket tossed over me.

I didn't know what time of day it was or even what day. The pictures hanging on the wall assured me I was still with George and Michelle.

Then an awful dread arose from inside, like something inside had oozed bile and bad blood. My stomach hurt, my chest felt tight, and the image of my father coughing blood returned.

Was there anything I could have done to stop the bleeding sooner? Could I have run faster to be near him? Why did it take so long for me to understand what was happening?

Was Dad alive?

I groaned and sobbed, coughing up thick saliva from my throat.

Michelle hurried into the room and sat beside me. "He made it through surgery, but he's still in the Intensive Care Unit."

"He is?"

"He has a long way to go to recover. He's not awake. I don't want to give you false hope. None of us knows when our time is up. But I've known your father for as long as I've known my husband, and David took on every challenge with everything he had available. He will not give up before his time. Your mother was the same way."

She put her arm around me, and that calmed me. Michelle's hair was natural, like an afro. She had enormous eyes and prominent cheekbones and wore pearl earrings and a necklace. I'd assumed it was morning, but her look made me wonder if it wasn't evening.

"You ready for breakfast?"

"I'm not hungry."

"You need to eat. Your father ain't saying much, but I'm sure he will appreciate feeling your hand squeeze his."

She brought me a tray of food. While I ate on the sofa, she brought out my Ashley wig on a Styrofoam head. I hadn't realized I wasn't wearing it.

"I combed it out for you," she said. "I have a few wigs myself, so I hope you don't mind. It needed a little attention."

My hands went up to my head. Then I decided I didn't care much if I looked like Joan but was living as Ashley. None of that mattered.

"George explained about your situation, about *Joan*, at least as much as he heard from your father."

"Oh."

"I did something similar when I was your age," she said. "Trying on different styles, seeing what worked, what I liked. It's all part of figuring out how to live."

When I peeked under the blanket, I realized I stank a bit and couldn't remember the last time I tidied up. While I was in the bathroom, the doorbell rang. When I came out, Britney was in the front room with Michelle.

"Hey Ash," Britney said. "Or should I say Joan?"

"Did you know?" I asked and pointed to my head.

She nodded. "My mom showed me a picture of Joan after the incident, and I realized it was you."

"You told her?"

"No," she said. "She still thinks Joan is in hiding. Sophie was pissing me off, so I kept your secret."

She offered me a bag. It was the weekender I'd packed with things from my father's office moments before he was shot in the face.

"Sophie said you can have this," Britney said.

"She said I can have it?"

"She doesn't want you back there."

"But I have a room there," I said. "I have things there."

"Yeah, well, she's taken her control issues up a notch."

"Control issues? She shot Dad in the face."

Britney nodded. "I'm sorry. For what it's worth, I gave her as much shit as possible about it and then she told me to leave, too."

"It's not like I want to go back there," I said, "but I don't like being forbidden."

I thought of my dad and panicked. I didn't know

what was happening and scrambled for my phone.

"Here you go," Michelle said, and handed it to me, charged up and wiped clean of my father's spilled blood. "But I called a little while ago and he was the same: unconscious and still in ICU."

"Thank you."

"They're tired of me already," Michelle said. "They offered to call if there was a change, but I'll keep calling."

Britney had also brought me clothes from my house —she and I traded keys for emergencies a year before— so I changed. "I found Joan's wardrobe," she said with a tinge of pride. "But the Ash look is probably better at the moment."

George arrived and settled himself in the chair across from the sofa. "There are a couple of things I'd like you to know."

"Have the police arrested Sophie?"

He shook his head. "From what I've gleaned, the Sheriff considers this an accident."

My stomach twisted, and I had to swallow to keep down the food. "There's no way it was an accident."

"Her story, as I understand it, is that your father offered her his gun for self-protection and it went off by mistake. She says she didn't know it was loaded."

"No," I said. "He went in there to tell her about Frank's embezzlement. He was going to tell her we were leaving because he suspected she was involved with Frank."

"They were involved?" Britney asked.

"They were fucking," I said. "That's what he thought.

And that she knew Frank was stealing from him."

Britney sobbed and sat on the sofa. I wondered if maybe I shouldn't have said it like that in front of her, but it was too-fucking-late.

George nodded, rocking slightly in his chair.

"Don't you care?" I said. "Doesn't anyone care she shot him in the face?"

"Of course we care," George said. "But your father and Sophie helped get that sheriff elected. He's a politician responsible for law and order. And Sophie has a plausible story."

"So she's going to get away with it?"

George looked at me for several seconds. "When your father recovers, he can tell us what happened."

# # # #

Britney and I were waiting at the hospital to visit my dad when a man in a police uniform approached. I was holding a magazine—not reading it, just rolling it up and unrolling it again, over and over.

"Are you Ashley Rice?"

I nodded.

"We've tried several times to reach you," he said. "We left voice mail and hand-delivered a note to your house."

I rolled up the magazine. "I've been here."

"How's your father doing?"

I couldn't speak, my throat closing before uttering a word. I unrolled the magazine enough to cover my face.

"He's out of surgery," Britney said. "His second surgery. We don't know how he is, but the doctor told us the surgery was a success. We have to wait for him to recover."

"I certainly don't mean to intrude, but we're trying to continue our investigation."

Britney sat up. "Exactly who are you?"

"I'm Detective Webber with the Washtenaw County Sheriff's Department."

"You're a detective?"

"Yes, ma'am."

"I thought detectives wore suits. You're dressed like a cop, except the uniform is brown."

"In the Sheriff's office, detectives wear these uniforms just like the deputies."

I patted Britney's arm. She'd been a jerk to many people before, but I wanted to hug her for trying to be a jerk to this detective.

"Okay," she said.

Webber seemed a little defensive, almost put out. "Even the Sheriff wears this uniform, but his is a little fancier."

"Fine, but we really don't want to talk to you."

"I only have a couple of questions for Miss Rice."

"It's fine," I said. "He already shit. May as well let him wipe."

He pondered this a moment and took a photo out of a leather folio, holding it up for me to see. "You changed your hair."

It was the photo the private investigator took outside Britney's coffee shop the day of the short-lived riot and shooting. In the picture, my father was next to me at the table on the sidewalk. "Can I have that?"

"It's part of my investigation," he said.

"I don't have a lot of photos of him," I said.

"Was your relationship with your father strained?"

I gripped the magazine with both hands, folding it. "Excuse me?"

"Like I said, we have a few questions."

"A question like 'who shot my father?' That I can answer: Sophie shot my father in the face."

He put the photo away. "Would you mind coming down to the Sheriff's office?"

Britney squeezed my arm. "I'll stay with Dad. It'll be fine. But you need George with you."

My hand went up to my head in a reflex. I'd developed a tic to check on my Ashley wig, worried it might be skewed. The wig was almost never out of place, but that's how the brain works when you worry about things too much. But I surprised myself because I wasn't wearing the wig. It was my short pixie cut in a fiery shade of red.

"I'm not going anywhere until we get to visit Dad."

The cop shifted his stance, squaring his shoulders. "I can drive you to the office now and have you back in an hour."

The magazine fell to the floor as I took off my glasses and covered my eyes with my hand. Ideas zapped around my head, images of Dad bleeding on the floor flashed between Sophie standing over us with a gun in her hand. I felt nauseous. I needed a Vernor's.

Ashley would probably go along as the officer

asked. But Joan might not.

"Leave me your card," I said. "My lawyer will schedule a time for us to talk."

The Sheriff's office was part of the sprawling county office campus between Ann Arbor and Ypsilanti. The Sheriff has just one building out of a dozen. You park, you walk, you hope you pick the right door.

Inside is a lobby where another brown uniform at a desk asks you about your business. Detective Webber showed up a couple of minutes later and escorted us to an interrogation room. Inside it was bare walls, tile floor, and only two chairs. I gasped and covered my stomach with my hands like someone had punched me.

George held out his arm, stopping me.

"You said you had some questions," he said. "A conference room would be more appropriate."

"None are available," Detective Weber said.

"Then we'll be back when one is available."

George led back towards the door.

"Hang on," Webber said. "Give me a minute."

He secured a conference room. This had carpeting, cushioned seats, and coffee and water service on a dolly. It didn't relieve me of my fear and anxiety, but it was better than that interrogation room.

I noticed there weren't any donuts and almost made a comment about it, but I thought better of it. That was a Joan idea followed by an Ashley decision.

Another detective, a woman in a brown uniform introduced as Detective Figueroa, joined detective

Webber. They sat across from us at the table.

"Is it true you were employed at HD Enterprises under a false identity?" Webber asked.

"Excuse me?"

George patted my hand. "Ms. Rice was not employed at HD Enterprises. Her legal entity, Joan Naumav LLC, was under contract to provide services."

"But she was there under a false identity?"

"What is the point of this questioning?" George asked. "Under what pretense have you asked Ms. Rice to be here?"

Webber jutted out his chin and raised his eyebrows. "Sophie Fox raised concerns about illegal activities at HD Enterprises—"

"Did she mention Frank Marshall's embezzlement?" I asked.

"She mentioned a cyber-attack resulting in a ransomware infestation disabling all the company's computers."

"Is this the only reason you asked her here?" George asked.

Detective Figueroa leaned forward. "We also want to take your statement regarding the events of the night your father was shot."

"You want to hear it now?" I asked. "Or do you have some other bullshit to ask me?"

Figueroa smiled. "If you're prepared to make your statement, proceed."

I glanced at George, and he nodded.

I told them how it happened, how my father wanted us to leave, that we packed, and we were going to go to a safe place, away from Sophie. That a minute or two after he left his office, there was a shot, and I found him bleeding from the mouth and called 911.

Figueroa finished her notes. "What next?"

"Sophie was holding the gun. She was calm as fuck and walked out of the room like nothing was wrong."

"She was probably in shock," Webber said.

"She shot him in cold blood."

"She doesn't deny holding the gun when it went off," Figueroa said.

"Are you going to arrest her?"

George whispered, "Easy."

"The District Attorney is gathering the facts about the case," Figueroa said.

"He's also interested in the cyber-attack," Webber said. "He may have more questions for you."

Out in the parking lot, I screamed until I cried. George held me until I calmed down.

"Yeah," George said. "I was afraid of some shit like that."

"What is the deal?"

"It all comes down to the District Attorney, and whether he wants to tackle this case."

"But she fucking shot him."

"It's a plausible story," George said. "Accidental shootings happen, and it was his gun. Also, people sometimes get away with murder."

"My dad's not dead."

"Of course. I didn't mean…"

"It's okay. I'm worried about him too."

"There's not much more we can do. There are half a dozen lesser charges he could bring against her, or he might do nothing."

"So she's going to get away with it?"

# # # #

I WAS AT THE HOSPITAL, NAPPING IN the visitor area, waiting for the next chance I could visit my dad. Intensive Care sucks because they limit the visiting hours and the number of visitors. I wasn't even supposed to hang around like I was, but the nurses talked to whoever was going to kick me out and let me stay. An orderly brought me a sandwich.

One of the ICU nurses coming off-duty, knowing I was probably still there, came to let me know he was doing better.

"He's still in a coma," she said, "but his numbers have stabilized."

I texted Britney. It was six o'clock in the morning, so I didn't expect a reply. Instead, I paced until they would allow one of us inside his room to visit. Like if he could just get out of Intensive Care, there'd be a chance he'd recover, wake up, and walk out of here.

That's all I wanted.

A little after seven, two people, an older man and a young woman, approached me in the visitor area. The woman carried a flower arrangement in a vase.

"Are you Ashley Rice?" the man asked.

"Are you cops?" I asked.

The woman chuckled. "What? No. What makes you think that?"

"If you were undercover cops, no one would suspect you."

"We work at HD Enterprises."

"Sorry. I'm a little punchy from lack of sleep."

"My name is Tyrian Copeland," the man said. "I'm the Union President. This is Vanessa Sweet. She's a union steward."

Tyrian was an older, bald man with an impish smile, a gray mustache, and deep-set eyes. He had light-brown skin that seemed golden on his cheeks and nose as he stood beneath the fluorescent lights.

Vanessa had an oval face and pale skin, pink across her cheeks and nose. The only makeup she wore was a touch of lip gloss a pale shade of red. She wore large glasses the same shade of red as her lip gloss, and a burgundy knit cap. An unruly bit of dark hair escaped from the cap.

I liked them both. They were sincerely concerned about my dad. Tyrian told me how supportive my mother had been of the union, how they all enjoyed negotiating the contract with her.

They wanted to know how I was doing and told me that everyone was hoping my dad would make a full recovery.

"He hasn't been the same since your mother died," Tyrian said, "but he's changed a lot of lives."

"For the better," Vanessa added.

Trying to be conversational, I reached into my barista bag of tricks and asked, "How are things down at the shop?"

Their expressions darkened. "Sophie has made some changes," Vanessa said.

"She's a bitch," Tyrian added.

"Wait," I said. "Sophie went to work? She only just shot my father three days ago."

"She's not working full days," Vanessa said. "She only came in a couple of hours."

Tyrian nodded. "Long enough to fire the production managers, demand overtime in the factory, and bring in a handful of contractors to run the floor."

"We complained, and she threatened layoffs."

"Oh my God," I said. "I'm so sorry."

"That's not the only reason we want your father to recover," Vanessa said.

"It's no surprise," Tyrian said. "In fact, she seems to relish being in charge."

"I'll help if I can," I said.

"Work is work," Tyrian said. "These things happen."

"Take care of yourself," Vanessa said, "so you can take care of your father."

34

I ʜᴇʟᴅ ᴍʏ ᴅᴀᴅ's ʜᴀɴᴅ ᴇᴀᴄʜ ᴇᴠᴇɴɪɴɢ while I watched the monitors plot his heartbeats and blood pressure. On the shelf behind the bed was an EEG tracking his brain activity. I liked to think of it tracking his thoughts.

The nurse told me to talk to him, that, even though he was in a coma, he could hear us, and might even process what we said.

"It's like a dream," she said, "but we don't know for sure. I like to think they hear us, so I chatter as much as possible, make it all seem normal, like someone you love is napping on the couch."

I used my barista skills to get started.

"How're you doing today, Dad? It's pretty nice out. I hope you wake up soon so we can go for a walk. You know the flowers in the Arb are coming in. I took a walk there today, but I know little about flowers."

Britney and I worked out that she would come in during the morning visiting hours and I would come in during the evening hours. The hospital only allowed one visitor per slot in the ICU, and there was also one in the afternoon that we kept open for George and Michelle.

Britney informed Sophie of the arrangement, but we weren't sure if she had visited yet. I could ask the nurses, I guess, but I didn't want to know. I wanted to think that she was done with my dad, and he could concentrate on getting better.

I certainly wouldn't bring up Sophie to my dad. So when the barista talk got old, I switched to Joan at the bar.

"Hey, this place sucks. Do you want to get out of here? Yeah? Good, because my friend needs that chair."

Even that got old. Truth is, I never enjoyed it. Talking like Joan was what I thought I was supposed to say to guys in bars.

I know my dad didn't like it because the numbers never budged. The pulse, blood pressure, and temperature stayed the same. When I squeezed his hand, he didn't squeeze back.

So, eventually, I talked about what I remembered when we were all happy.

"Do you remember how the upstairs of the house in Ringerton had cubbies in the eaves? You showed me how to pull a hunk of the wall away and that's where we stored my games, and the Christmas decorations, and old stuff that you and Mom had as kids.

"I used to take a flashlight and read in there. Even though I had my own room, and no one bothered me, I still liked the idea of having this secret place all to myself. The spider webs didn't bug me, or the dust or the weird smells. I enjoyed knowing I was safe in a secret place with you and Mom downstairs.

"I hated the basement. The spider webs seemed so much worse down there, and the stuff stored there seemed more like junk, and then I realized a lot of it had come with the house and we hadn't gotten around to getting rid of it yet.

"Then it wasn't so bad and I poked around in the boxes.

"Remember when I found a box of old flash bulbs? I guess they were really old because inside each bulb was a ball of fine wire. You showed me how to use a couple of stacked batteries and aluminum foil to fire them. We'd turn out the lights in the basement and light up the entire room for an instant, and then there was the purple image in my eyes, like glancing at the sun.

"You let me do it twice, but then you made me promise not to do it if you weren't there because you wanted nothing to happen to me. And I didn't, because I felt loved and secure with you."

There was one evening when I know he heard me, because his pulse sped up, and the lines on the EEG moved more than usual.

It was when I said, "I never talked to you or Mom about when I was born. I guess there are pictures and videos somewhere, but I wish I'd asked.

"I bet I was born here, in this hospital. Maybe not in this part, but close by.

"Even when Mom was here for her treatments, I wish I'd asked her then."

DAVID

THEY WERE AT THE HOUSE IN Ringerton on a Friday night. It was dark, but David wasn't sure about the time. He knew it was the end of the day because they'd eaten supper, piled the dishes in the sink, and started up the stairs.

"Katie can handle the Finance team," Heather said. "We should promote her to a director level, or something like that. Give her more money than she can get anywhere else in Michigan."

"She's that good?" he asked. But he knew the answer. They were pregnant, then. He knew Katie would do the job while Heather was out on maternity leave and for the next four years after that, until, finally, she got an offer they couldn't match.

He knew it was a memory playing out as a dream, and that he was asleep. But David was fine with it. He didn't want to wake up and spoil the memory because he hadn't thought of this moment in a long time.

"We need someone to deal with all the computer issues," she said, and paused a few steps short of the second floor to catch her breath. "Wow, I can't wait until our little angel arrives."

"What's this?"

David noticed something on the step below Heather's feet. It was like a blob of gelatin and reflected the light. He touched it and was repulsed.

"That's my mucous plug," Heather said, looking down from above.

"Where the hell did it come from?"

"Where the hell do you think?"

"What does it mean?" David asked.

"I think it means my water is going to break soon."

They checked Heather's bag and got ready for bed, but didn't expect to sleep much. A few seconds into brushing her teeth, her water broke and the first contraction started.

David called the doctor, who told them to wait until the contractions were closer.

At the hospital, the nurses were calm and matter-of-fact. David was out of his element, unable to recite a formula that would explain why it took so long for their baby to be born. Heather wasn't calm. It was more like a contained fury, and David didn't know how to help.

The epidural was administered and then Heather calmed down. The labor dragged on for hours, through all the bad television on Saturday mornings, back when the hospital didn't spring for premium channels.

At four in the afternoon, the doctor inserted his hand and measured the dilation with the tips of his fingers, declaring she was ready to push.

The rest was a blur, but he watched as their angel's head crowned and then, in a magnificently messy act of maternity, emerged from Heather.

"Do we have a name?" a nurse asked.

"Ashley," Heather said.

David said her name, but he was crying.

He was crying even as he dreamed, and knew it was a memory, but also knew it was the happiest moment of his life.

35

SOPHIE

Sophie relied on her attorney, John Beckley, to plan with the hospital for discreet visits. He explained how he used his connection to the university's president, and the dean of the school of medicine, to make it happen. Sophie thanked him, but the look of quiet despair in his eyes was not her problem. It wasn't her fault he longed for her validation.

She had much bigger problems. That's why she, worried about news reporters staking it out, ready to ambush her with unfortunate questions, needed Beckley in this moment.

The optics of the situation were terrible.

Of course, she hadn't *wanted* to shoot David. There was no good way to answer that question, so she would do everything possible to avoid being asked.

A terrible accident occurred; the only thing that mattered was supporting David's full recovery.

She dressed conservatively in off-white or bone, avoiding black and even gray. She also kept outfits simple, lest someone comments on the level of fashion on display. She toyed with wearing a wig. It had been truly shocking how Ashley had fooled her, so why not do the same now to avoid attention?

If someone at the hospital tipped off a reporter, there's no telling how they'd frame her with a disguise story. Shame? Admission of guilt? Mental instability?

Beckley secured a special ID card that allowed Sophie to use the employee entrance on the side. The first visit, Beckley had been there to show her the path through the building: down the main hall, through the double-doors on the left, then an immediate right to the secret elevator and up to Intensive Care.

Now she breezed in with authority, confident that everyone understood their place.

Sophie made a point of looking at the nurse's station, daring their disapproving looks. Once settled in the chair beside David's bed, she felt in control, as if this were her place to be, and no one would dare suggest otherwise.

"David, darling," she began each time, "it's me, your beloved Sophie."

She gave his hand a squeeze and resettled herself in the chair. The first few days, it'd been tough to think of what to say, but now she felt like her old self, in control.

"I've made changes at the office, darling. It's entirely possible this personal setback may work out for the company, profit-wise. I know you resisted some of my ideas, but the results will bear out.

"I admit, though, the burden of leadership is not light. My darling, you so often made it look easy. I really never appreciated all that you did. So get better soon and we'll compare notes.

"I know you'll like how I took care of that mess with Frank in Finance, and the rest of it. No need to dredge up that, right Darling?"

Sophie leaned forward and patted his hand. She knew she was saying the right things, but wasn't sure it sounded right. Without a reaction from David's face, there was nowhere to go with the conversation and eek out his feelings about things.

She cast a glance about for a magazine, but there were none. She supposed it was a consequence of Intensive Care that not even flowers were allowed in the room.

"Keep getting better, Darling. We'll get you to a regular room and then we can make things a bit more homey."

A foul thought crossed her mind. Did she want him to recover? She rather enjoyed being in charge, and in just these past few days, there had been inquiries from three different companies looking to partner, license their technology, or acquire them. David, of course, would resist all this, as he had for years. But these were exciting opportunities.

Then there was the preposterous suggestion his daughter made. David wanting to maintain ownership of the company he founded was one thing, but the child's idea of simply giving it all away was laughable.

Sophie wasn't exactly sure what she was thinking when she pulled the trigger that day, but not that she wanted to kill. But all of it—the company, the foolishness with Frank, the stealing, the family—was all jumbled up in that moment as he sat down with a decision that made no sense. It was simply not true that she had wanted her husband dead.

What she had wanted was for David to go on being the entrepreneur she fell in love with. It just worked out that she had to shoot him for that to happen. There was no reason anything had to change. Not even the thing with Frank had altered her feelings for David, at least not in any meaningful way. She still loved him as much as she did when they married.

Somehow, his daughter got inside his head and set him down a path of ruination.

Sophie had hoped the ransomware incident would set David's resolve against any further distractions. It could have been a blessing. Instead, it exposed his one vulnerability, and weakened his decision-making.

Besides, any fool who understood all the ramifications would see that David's death would entwine her with Ashley in a legal struggle for years. She'd rather mud wrestle that silly child than deal with her claims on David's estate and the company.

"And here you are in a kind of limbo, Darling," she said. "But you take all the time you need to get better."

She'd said it with a hint of sarcasm, but now another thought crossed her mind.

Sophie stood and kissed David on the forehead. She leaned close to his ear and whispered, "Don't worry about me. I'm going to stay strong while you're busy healing."

DAVID

DAVID KEPT MOVING FROM HIS OFFICE at the house to Sophie's office and thinking with each move that he'd forgotten something. Was it his briefcase? Was it his lunch? Was he supposed to be somewhere else?

He thought of Heather, how happy he was that they married, and then found himself in Sophie's office stricken with guilt and shame for having married Sophie while still married to Heather. How could he have forgotten Heather?

But he hadn't forgotten Heather. She died, and that's why he married Sophie.

Then he was in his office again, presumably to get his briefcase, and saw Ashley. Did she know her mother had died? Was he going to tell her? And would she be mad about Sophie?

As this loop repeated, he realized he was in a dream because he was not the sort of person to forget about his wife and go off to marry someone else. There was no reason to feel shame or guilt.

He left Ashley in his office and went into another room, but this time it was Heather's room, in hospice. Ashley was there on the other side of the bed and they each held one of Heather's hands.

"Promise me," Heather said.

"I promise," David said.

He knew what he'd forgotten. The shame and guilt rushed over him and it wasn't a dream anymore but a nightmare. He tried to scream, but he couldn't talk.

He wanted to wake up but knew he'd be trapped there forever with the shame and guilt pulling him down into the darkness.

ASHLEY

I WAS WITH MY DAD FOR a couple of hours when I realized this routine had become a kind of new normal for me. I'd moved some of my stuff into Britney's condominium, and I slept there, had breakfast with her —not an actual meal, because she ate little food in the morning, but I made tea and coffee for us. I stayed at her place while she went to visit Dad.

She called after the visit to tell me how Dad was doing.

I walked around Ann Arbor to distract myself during the afternoon. If George was going to visit, he'd let me know and he, too, called after seeing Dad.

I went over to George and Michelle's for supper around five. After that, I visited Dad.

Despite the terrible situation, it made the day bearable. After a week, it felt like what we'd be doing for a while.

This day, though, George told me on the phone that he crossed paths with Sophie as he left. "She said hello," he said, "but she wasn't chatty."

"Do you think that's good for Dad?" I had butterflies in my stomach. The hatred for Sophie clashing with the concern for my father. I was confused, but still hoping for anything like good news.

"I don't know, but let me know how he is tonight."

When I visited, there was more color in my father's face, which I took as a positive change. I held his hand, hoping for something, but it was limp. Still, I squeezed it when I needed to remind myself he was still with me.

My mind blipped and for a few seconds, I wasn't sure how long this had been going on. What day of the week was it? When had he been shot? Was it weeks or a month?

Then I wondered how long this might go on. There are stories you hear about people being in a coma for weeks or months. Usually, those stories don't end well. But some people wake up. I thought it might still have a happy ending.

I noticed his pulse was up slightly, to around eighty-seven beats per minute, and his temperature was up almost two degrees. I hit the button for the nurse.

The nurse reviewed the numbers. It was the first nurse I met there, the one who coached me on talking to dad. I was happy it was her. Somehow, I felt more secure with her on duty.

"I'll call the doctor," she said. "The blood pressure is fine, so he might have an infection."

"Is that bad?"

"Probably not. But we're going to take care of him."

She didn't sound worried, but she didn't sound confident, either. I spiraled into that despair again, that maybe this would be it, and all the mysteries inside him would be gone forever.

There was a quick burst of activity when the nurse returned and took a blood sample from his intravenous tube. She checked all the sensors to make sure they were attached. Finally, she injected something into the IV.

"We're giving him something for the fever to make

sure he's comfortable, but we won't know for a while what it is."

"Thank you."

It was just me and Dad. I took his hand and squeezed it. Those numbers were still elevated, and his breathing seemed more rapid. I felt as if he was struggling.

I cried, feeling like the surrounding light was fading as pressure built around my chest. But I remembered I was here for him, and I was his only connection to the outside world at the moment.

"Dad, I don't want you to worry about anything. I pushed you too hard about the company and what Mom wanted. I know you had more on your mind than I knew about, and I should have been patient and understanding.

"What I want now is for you to rest and get better.

"Mom loved you and I love you. Britney loves you. George and Michelle love you. Your employees love you. There are hundreds of people who love you and want you to get better.

"So rest, and know that you're loved."

Tears ran down my cheek, but I'd stopped sobbing. I felt like I hadn't told him how much I loved him enough, and that the past few weeks were a mess because of me. But I didn't want him to know I was upset.

I pulled it together as best I could and kissed him on the forehead again.

"I love you more than anything in this world."

DAVID

Dᴀᴠɪᴅ ꜰᴏᴜɴᴅ ʜɪᴍꜱᴇʟꜰ ɪɴꜱɪᴅᴇ ᴛʜᴇ ʜᴏᴜꜱᴇ in Ringerton at the back door, looking at the yard. Heather was pushing Ashley on the swing he rigged with a rope tied to the branch of the oak tree. The two lengths of rope were different, so the swing twisted with each push, but Ashley squealed with delight.

Heather laughed.

Seeing David, she waved to him. "Come on. Your turn to push."

He walked across the yard bathed in light toward the shade of the oak. He knew there was work back inside—for the company, repairs to the house—but that would be alright. He was going to be with his family.

Ashley's laughter blended with Heather's, and he laughed as well.

It was going to be alright.

ASHLEY

THE NEXT MORNING, BRITNEY MADE US smoothies. It was soy milk, frozen berries, and a scoop of plant-based protein powder. She also threw a handful of kale in for texture, I guess. It was fine for her. She still played tennis twice a week and ran three miles to calm herself down on her "off" days. I was grateful for her company, so I was fine with any food.

"I'm going to work late, again," she said as she packed her lunch. "I actually enjoy this late start at the office because people leave me alone."

Her phone rang, and she picked up before I could respond.

"Hey Sophie," she said and rolled her eyes. Then she sat down on the kitchen stool and lowered her gaze. "Okay," she said. "Got it. Right. Of course. Thanks for letting us know."

It didn't seem like good news.

"Dad's status changed," she said. "He had trouble breathing during the night and his blood pressure was low. They called Sophie, and she told them to do whatever was necessary to save him."

I was sobbing. Once again, the light was fading and pressure built on my chest. Crying relieved the pressure a little. Britney held me and I felt more at ease with the bad news.

"He's stable now," she said through the sobs. "He's on a ventilator."

36

SOPHIE

FROM HER UPSTAIRS OFFICE, SOPHIE WATCHED as Frank's car approached the front of the house. The new intercom gadget on her desk chirped, and Sophie pressed the button.

"Are you expecting a visitor?" Carl, the security guard on duty, asked.

"I'm expecting a Frank Marshall," she said. "Verify his identity."

"Will do."

Her lawyer, Beckley, sat in the seat in front of the desk. His soft, pale face reminded her of a deep-sea fish, the ones that live their entire lives in total darkness. His mouth was open slightly. His gray hair was unkempt and too long, likely an attempt to compensate for its thinning. At least there was no risk of ever being attracted to this man.

"I'd like you to explain the agreement to Frank," Sophie said. "I don't want there to be any misunderstanding."

"Of course."

As Beckley gathered together the papers they'd been discussing, Frank came in.

"What the hell is with the security guy?" he asked. "Since when do I have to show ID to get in here?"

"You can't be too careful these days," Sophie said. "You had an intruder the week before last."

"Yeah," Frank said. "It was your step-kid."

"My point exactly."

Frank unbuttoned his jacket, sat down, and shot a glance at Beckley but didn't return the lawyer's polite smile. "How's Dave doing?"

"Not good," Sophie said. "I'm afraid his condition worsened a bit. We almost lost him, but God bless those miracle workers."

"Is he going to recover?"

Sophie looked at Beckley, who perked up.

"At the moment, Mr. Rice needs help with breathing, and his brain activity has, sadly, stopped."

"Oh, shit."

"But he's still with us," Sophie said. "And I'm going to take good care of the company so that, if he recovers, he can step back into the leadership role."

Frank got himself an energy drink from the mini-fridge. "You won't pull the plug?"

Sophie heaved a sigh. "Frank, I'm too exhausted to put up with your ham-fisted, insensitive comments. This is my husband you're talking about."

Frank cracked open the energy drink and took a sip. "You probably get charged with manslaughter if he dies?"

"Excuse me," Beckley said, surprising Sophie with

the tense expression on his otherwise flaccid face. "That is a subject we will not discuss."

"Hey, sorry. I thought this was a business discussion."

"It's a family matter," she said. "You understand?"

Frank nodded.

Beckley placed a manila folder on the desk. "About the matter—"

Sophie slapped her hand on the folder. "Would you excuse us? I'd like a few minutes with Frank, alone."

Beckley got up and backed out of the office, closing the door as he left.

Sophie pulled the manila folder to her side of the desk. "Do you know what this is about?"

"The money," Frank said.

"It's also about us," Sophie said.

Frank nodded.

"I cared about you," she said. "You know that, right?"

"I knew that."

"But you took up with that young thing."

"Nikki."

"She seems more like Jared's type."

"It surprised me she was interested in me," Frank said.

"Tell me: did she know you were taking money from the company? Was that part of the attraction?"

"Maybe a little."

Sophie patted the folder. "David's private investigator has it all figured out. I could just take it to the District Attorney."

"I'll pay it all back."

"I would have let you keep it," she said. "Except for

that girl."

"Honestly," Frank said, "I thought you were done with me."

"Maybe I was, but you're going to pay back every cent."

"With interest?"

"No," Sophie said. "I'll wave the interest charges as a farewell gift."

"Thank you."

She called for Beckley to return, and the lawyer took back the manila folder and opened it.

"One second," Frank said. "So, where did it happen?"

"Where did what happen?" Sophie asked.

"Where did you shoot him?"

"I didn't *shoot* him."

"No?"

Beckley cleared his throat. "There was an accidental discharge of the weapon that, sadly, injured Mr. Rice."

Frank nodded at Beckley. "Okay, where did the accidental discharge of the weapon happen?"

Sophie pushed her eyeglasses to the top of her head. "Right where you're sitting."

Frank looked down at the floor.

"I had the carpets replaced," Sophie said. "And I'll have you know the Sheriff returned both handguns."

Frank raised his hands in mock surrender and leaned back in the chair. "Good to know."

ASHLEY

We went directly to the hospital to see our dad. We were both allowed into his room. The nurse was nice and gentle about the situation, but I could sense that her edge of worry was gone. She seemed sorry for us, sympathetic. The optimism was gone and, with it, our hope.

Still, we each took a hand and talked to him, trying to sound upbeat. The ventilator stood guard, keeping us from getting too close to Dad.

After a couple of minutes, our forced, upbeat chatter subsided. We sat there on either side of the bed, each staring at some point close to Dad, but not directly at him. The ventilator hissed, clicked and whirred each second, a ghastly clock passing time.

I felt like I'd gone for a long walk and lost my way. I was far from where I wanted to be, dark clouds were pressing in, and I was unsure what would be best.

The worst part was that I wasn't worried or concerned about myself. I didn't cry; I was beyond that point. Maybe the feeling wasn't of being lost, but of having found my way back to a place I didn't like: sitting next to a parent on their deathbed.

The nurse returned at some point and asked, "Do you need anything?"

"Can we talk to his doctor?" Britney asked.

The nurse nodded and left the room.

A few minutes later, a woman wearing a jacket and slacks came in. She had a leather folder under her arm and extended her hand to greet us.

"I'm Nadine Green," she said. "I'm a Patient Care Caseworker."

"No offense," I said, "but can we talk to the doctor?"

"Let's talk in the lounge."

She led us down the hall, out of Intensive Care, to a room furnished like a family room. She sat on a chair and we took the sofa.

"In cases such as your father," she said, "I coordinate care between the doctors and insurance, and also the next of kin."

"Yeah," I said. "So what's next?"

"I'm afraid your father has taken a turn down a challenging path for successful treatment."

I wasn't sure what I hated more: her choice of words or the look of trained compassion on her face. Like, I got that she had to do this, probably twice a week, but it hurt worse because of that. I guess I don't know how you're supposed to discuss this, but I knew this was a poor start.

"Why can't the doctors operate again? Is it bleeding, or is it swelling, or is it the infection?"

"It's likely all three," she said. "The doctor gave a zero chance for success."

"Can we get another opinion?" Britney asked.

"I have to tell you," Nadine said, "the doctors don't consider this a persistent vegetative state. They consider him to be brain dead."

"Then we need another doctor," I said.

Nadine patted the notebook in her lap. "Your father named his wife, Sophie Fox, as his health care proxy.

We must abide by her decision."

We sat with Dad for half an hour before my anger subsided. Britney, on the other side of his bed, took his hand and sighed.

I did the same. "We need to talk to George."

George and Michelle arrived and hugged us, held Dad's hands, patted his shoulder. While Michelle stayed with Dad, we went with George to the lounge.

"You could fight her status," he said, "but that document holds considerable weight."

"So there's nothing we can do?"

George rocked a bit in his chair. "What is it you want to do?"

"Get another doctor in here," Britney said.

"These are some of the finest doctors in the state, possibly in the Midwest, right in this building. I'm sure we could find one, somewhere, who would take your side in the discussion, but what is it you want to do?"

"I want my dad to get the best care possible," I said.

George nodded. "This breaks my heart, but I don't think he's coming back from this."

I cried then, loudly and for a long time. Worse, even, than after the shooting. It was like I'd been holding back because of some slim possibility of his recovery, but hearing George say that broke the dam.

Britney was right there with me.

Finally, exhausted and out of tears for the moment, I cleared my throat. "So, when will it happen?"

George said nothing.

Finally, Britney spoke up. "I'll talk to Sophie."

SOPHIE

SOPHIE WAS ON THE TENNIS COURT returning balls fired from the machine across the net. Clyde, dressed in a black golf shirt and black slacks stood behind the ball machine. He turned off the machine and walked to the net.

"Visitor," he said.

"That's Britney," she said. "You may stand down."

"What's with your coach?" Britney asked.

"That's Clyde," Sophie said. She moved her feet to practice her backhand swing. "He's with security. He chose that spot as his vantage point."

"You have two full-time security agents?"

Sophie snapped her fingers and Clyde restarted the machine. "Can't be too careful."

"Is tennis part of the mourning process?"

Sophie turned and strode over to where Britney stood at the entrance to the courts, ignoring the balls sailing over the net every five seconds.

"Physical activity helps me sleep, lightens my mood."

"Okay."

"Some aspects of life go on, even during difficult and tragic times."

"Yes," Britney said. "I'm sorry."

"Would you have me cover the mirrors and mope around in black?"

"No. I shouldn't have said that. Black makes you look pale and drained."

Sophie waved her racket at Clyde, who nodded and turned off the ball machine.

"Exactly, my dear," Sophie said. "Besides, David isn't dead. I'm not mourning, but processing grief."

"Can we go inside and talk in private?"

Sophie poured two smoothies, and they sat in the kitchen with Clyde out of sight. Sophie wasn't too worried about his overhearing this conversation—this security company was well-regarded—but she wanted Britney to be at ease.

"What is it, my dear?"

"It's David, of course," Britney said. "What are your intentions?"

Sophie sipped her drink and swallowed. "It's my duty to provide him the best care possible."

"The case manager, or whatever the hell she is, said there's no chance of recovery."

"Oh, there's always a chance."

"You'll leave him on that respirator indefinitely?"

Sophie nodded and took another drink.

"But indefinitely?" Britney asked. "I think it's cruel."

"It's not cruel. Not when it's someone you love."

Britney placed a hand on her drink and moved it closer, pushed it away, released it. In a whisper, she asked, "Are you worried they'll charge you with murder when he dies?"

Sophie shook her head. "What happened was an accident. I have nothing to worry about beyond the heavy feeling of tragic, senseless loss."

"I don't think you're being fair to dad."

"I'm loving him in the best way I know how."

"How long will you let this go on?"

Sophie's eyebrows scrunched down. "I'm running his business, which is perhaps the best way to honor his life and keep his memory alive. Not many people could do what I'm doing right now. I should think you'd appreciate my service to that element of your stepfather's life."

"We hate seeing him in this condition," Britney said. "He deserves to rest."

"None of this would have happened if Ashley, or Joan—whatever she's going by at the moment—hadn't committed those stupid felony crimes against the company. If anyone is to blame for this mess, it's her."

ASHLEY

BRITNEY AND I WENT TO THE hospital and sat with dad, not sure what we should do, or if there was anything we could do. His situation didn't change, his fate seemed sealed. He would linger here, not technically dead but not really alive, until Sophie was done with him.

I invited Britney to the cemetery to talk about Dad's situation.

It was a warm afternoon. I guess it was July. There hadn't been rain in a while and the grass was mostly brown. The black birds lined up in the tall grass, shouting at each other. Across the cemetery, I noticed a woodchuck nibbling on something.

Mom's grave marker reflected the sun where I stood, and I shielded my eyes. "Have I told you I talk to her?"

"Who?" Britney asked.

"My mom."

Britney shielded her eyes from the reflection. "Okay."

"But I don't have to talk. I think about her, and I hear her voice."

"You're sure it's her?"

"I'm sure."

"If Sophie could do that, get inside my head, I might be okay with her shooting me instead."

I smiled. Britney was there with me, doing her best to help me.

"Sorry," she said. "I'll shut up now."

A warm breeze stirred up the leaves on the tree. In the west, a dark cloud approached, but it didn't threaten to rain.

I thought about my dad in the hospital. I didn't know what to do to help him, or even what was the right thing to do. Should I start a lawsuit and publicly humiliate Sophie? Should I hit her? Or should I wait?

I heard my mother say, "Surrender."

Britney's eyes opened wide and her mouth opened.

"Did you hear it?" I asked.

"No," she said. "You look like you heard something."

I didn't believe her, but I nodded.

"What do we do?"

"Surrender."

"What does 'surrender' mean?" Britney asked.

"I think I know," I said. "Let's go talk to George."

We met in George's office: me, Britney, George, Sophie and her lawyer, all seated around the conference room table. George had water and coffee, but no other refreshments. It was strictly business.

Sophie scrutinized the furnishings and decor of the office as her lawyer poured a glass of water for her. "All these years of practice and this is what you have to show for it?"

"My office is not to your liking?" George asked in a flat tone.

"Maybe it's a cultural thing," she said. "Where did you and David grow up?"

"Livonia."

She nodded. "Livonia."

"Sophie," I said. "I will release all claims to HD Enterprises."

"Oh?" She sipped the water, then pushed it away while making a face, feigning confusion.

"I also don't want any of my father's fortune when he passes. I will release all claims to anything he has designated as my inheritance in his Last Will and Testament."

Sophie raised an eyebrow. "After what you did to our company, at least you're consistent. Too bad he's not here to suffer the blow from this rejection of his love."

George had advised me not to engage in any petty argument she might draw me into, so I waited.

Sophie snapped her fingers at her lawyer. "What is this? Are you trying to buy me off so I don't pursue criminal charges?"

"There is a quid pro quo," George said.

"Ooh, lawyerly talk," Sophie said. "This should be rich."

"I want to be designated as my father's medical proxy and guardian, and to decide all matters about his funeral and burial."

"You want him dead."

"I want him to rest."

Sophie tapped a nail on the table. "You dragged me out to Plymouth to tell me I'm not caring for my husband. Or is there some nefarious purpose? Is this being recorded?"

I held up my index finger. "I will also swear out a

statement that I believe my father's death was an accident, and that I hold no ill-will towards you. I promise to make no statements, public or private, about the matter. Should the police ever charge you with any crime related to the incident, I'll testify that it was an accident."

Sophie glanced at her lawyer and rolled her eyes. "Talk is cheap."

"We can work out the details," George said. "I can work with Mr. Beckley, or someone else if you'd rather."

"I warn you," Sophie said and glanced at her lawyer, "he may not look like much, but he's a hell of a negotiator."

37

ASHLEY

For two days, Britney and I swapped stories as we sat beside Dad at the hospital. I told Britney about growing up in Ringerton. Britney told me about *her* father, and what Sophie was like back then (not terribly different from how she was when I knew her). On the second day, we talked mostly about Dad, and all the good things he did for us: the driving lessons, the help with school, and his jokes.

While we did that, George and Beckley negotiated. It was late afternoon of the second day when Sophie and I signed the agreement, and the hospital recognized me as my father's medical proxy and guardian.

On the third day, after a consultation with Dad's case manager, we removed my dad from life support. The ventilator tube was removed, and the machine moved out of the way so we could be close.

I expected it to be surreal, like I wouldn't believe what was happening. Instead, it was hyper-real. I heard every breath taken in the room. I heard the shuffle of feet across the tile floor. I noticed when Britney scratched her nose. The way George carefully cleared his throat, covering his mouth with the crook of his arm while also turning away to be as discreet as possible.

I held Dad's hand and watched him, hoping he might somehow take a breath, open his eyes and call my name. Anything, really.

Instead, I saw him grow still. His face grew a shade paler. His hand felt half an ounce heavier in mine.

With me, Britney, George and Michelle at his bedside, David Rice died at 2:43 p.m. on July 10th. I think it was a Thursday.

Sophie was in the room. By agreement, George and Michelle stepped into the hall. Britney and I stood near the door, and Sophie spent as much time as she wanted with Dad.

She left after two minutes without saying a word.

I held the memorial service at a Lutheran church. We never went to services there but attended a few picnics —the three of us: me, Dad and Mom—and I knew the pastor liked Dad.

The casket was in the lobby and Dad looked fine, I guess, as far as people in caskets go. The weeks in the hospital probably didn't help. His face was puffy and made up. His hands folded across his stomach.

I didn't think I could touch him, but Britney rested her hand on Dad's arm and that gave me courage. I gave his hand a squeeze.

Sophie patted the edge of the casket and moved on.

The line of people waiting to pay their respects went into the parking lot and stretched around the church. Britney and I were on one side of the casket and all those people were going to come in and tell me how sorry they were.

At first, I was overwhelmed, close to a panic attack. Britney hugged people and shook hands like a pro. She pulled me aside, held me, and said, "Let Joan deal with these people."

I was fine after that. Most of the people were sad. Some were concerned for me, or Britney, or both. Some had forgotten I existed, or never knew me.

It was so weird and heartbreaking as they flowed past for two straight hours.

Kirsten and Julie came, and I burst into tears while hugging them. But that felt good to cry like that with friends.

Sophie was on the other side of the casket. Had I banished her, it would have been weirder. As it was, she didn't talk to us. She didn't even look at us.

Once the casket was closed and wheeled into the nave, Sophie sat in the first row with her lawyer. Britney and I sat behind her, with George and Michelle beside us.

The rest of the pews in the nave were packed. People stood along the side and in the lobby, looking on through the windows. Nearly all the HD Enterprises employees were there: his friends from college, my mom's friends from all over the community, and people I'd never seen or heard of.

The pastor did a marvelous job, and George delivered a hell of a eulogy, bidding his friend goodbye.

We interred my father at the cemetery beside my mother. It was a lovely day, and I was happy that so many people had a chance to enjoy the view of little Ringerton from this vantage. There was a cool breeze coming from over the water, cumulus clouds overhead, and sunshine warming our faces.

Near the end of the service, after the Lutheran pastor read something from the Bible, we began a procession to pass by the coffin and lay flowers on it. As we stood in front of our seats while the other attendees walked past the casket, raindrops fell. Above us was a blue sky —it was a sun-shower. The sunlight glinted off the falling rain, sparkling like diamonds.

I lifted my face and smiled. Britney looked up as well. Within seconds, the procession halted and everyone stood looking up into the sun-shower.

Britney and I laughed. I'm not sure who started, but others joined. Kirsten smiled as she watched me laugh, then laughter overtook her, as well. It just seemed to happen—a spontaneous outburst of joy—like the sparkling rain falling from a blue sky.

SOPHIE

Sᴏᴘʜɪᴇ ʜᴏsᴛᴇᴅ ᴀ ᴍᴇᴍᴏʀɪᴀʟ ɢᴀᴛʜᴇʀɪɴɢ ꜰᴏʀ her late husband at Wagner's Inn, a reputable place with traditional decor able to accommodate a sizable crowd. She directed Gail, her secretary, to make the arrangements and to notify people. All managers, directors, and vice presidents were expected to attend. Their assistants would be welcome, but weren't required to attend.

Sophie had a list of other individuals, elected officials to whom she gave substantial donations, members of the various non-profits to which she donated respectable amounts, that were also to be invited.

She was stumped when Gail asked, "What about your friends?"

She thought of her sorority sisters and maid of honor from her first wedding, but couldn't recall their names. "I'll get you the list," Sophie said.

This had all happened the afternoon that David passed. Sophie had returned to the house, told Clyde to check the rooms, and then sent him outside to stand guard or whatever. She wanted to be alone.

Sophie wandered from her office down to David's office and back up again. Not sure what to do with herself, she kept wandering until she arrived in the front room. Her wedding photo with David hung above the table, where several framed wedding pictures stood: she and David dancing; she and David at the table; she and David with Governor Snyder, whom she met through her first husband. Sophie gave plenty of money to the governor's PAC, and yet he'd only given her a case of domestic wine—from Michigan, no less—as a wedding gift.

Their wedding was on the small side, with only a hundred of their closest associates. David had wanted to invite his first wife's relations, but Sophie had told him no. The attendees were mostly from Sophie's life, and David hadn't seemed to mind.

That warm feeling of adoration had been wonderful. Even as they honeymooned in the Aegean, she fondly recalled the nice things people said to them.

That, she realized, was what she wanted for David's memorial: a hundred friends gathered together to eat and remember David.

The arrangements were made, and the invitations sent out before Ashley put David in the ground. It had surprised Sophie to see some people invited to her private memorial also in attendance at the Lutheran church and at the cemetery. She didn't begrudge them. It simply wasn't a thing she would have done if the situation was reversed. She had to be there. They had a choice.

They held the memorial dinner the Saturday following David's burial. Clyde pulled the XT6 up to the front door. Beckley, who had been waiting for her arrival, held the door open.

"Everything ready?" she asked.

Gail, who was with the hostess, nodded. "We're in The Atrium. The evening light is gorgeous today."

Sophie smiled and walked in the direction Gail had pointed.

The Atrium was stunning. High above, in the glass-paneled ceiling, the moon was moored in a blue sky as the sun hovered an inch above the trees. Along the sides of the atrium, the lush vegetation glowed with up-lighting from the garden beds. In the middle of the room, twenty-four round tables were set out for a traditional meal. At Gail's suggestion, there was a sixth chair at each table so that Sophie could visit them without disturbing anyone's place.

She placed her handbag at the head table and made her way to the bar in the corner.

"Gin and tonic," she said. "Lemon twist."

The bartender seemed young enough to still be in college. He wore a black shirt, had thick brown hair, and a goofy smile on his face, but he chose the correct brand of gin, Bombay, and was generous with the pour.

She snapped her fingers for another, thanked him with a smile and wandered back to the table where Gail and Beckley were in conversation.

"Is everything ready?" she asked. "You'd tell me if there were a problem."

"I'm worried about the attendance," Gail said.

Two dozen people milled about the side of the room, admiring the wedding photos displayed on a table.

"What time is it?"

"It's time."

"Let's wait a few. Perhaps people are worried about being early."

Sophie finished her first drink and carried the second towards the guests at the photo table. Although they were managers and directors at the company, Sophie barely recognized half. She thanked a few for coming and accepted their compliments on the photos.

"He was a handsome man and a wonderful husband," she said. "We'll all miss him."

At the first whiff of awkward silence, Sophie returned to Gail and Beckley. "Well?"

"This is it."

"You'd better make some calls."

Gail froze for a moment. She put down her glass of wine and stepped out into the hallway.

Sophie glared at Beckley. He avoided eye contact by looking up at the moon, the guests, and at the door. Eventually, he looked at Sophie.

"I'm sure it's nothing personal," he said. "Just one of those scheduling things."

"This is your fault," she hissed. "You negotiated the deal. You granted Ashley full control of the memorial and the burial."

"I thought you thought this was a good deal."

"Look at it," she said. "Does this look like a good deal?"

Beckley shook his head.

"You need to think of something."

He looked at the doors again as if hoping to see a crowd arrive to save him.

"Not now, you fool. Think of some other way to get these people to a memorial. We have to end this embarrassment and come up with a rescheduled event.

It has to be plausible. And you have to make them understand they need to attend. This is not acceptable."

He nodded. "Of course."

"You can tell me about it in the morning," she said. "I'm going to deal with her myself."

She grabbed her bag and found Gail in the hallway, backing her against the wall.

"That God damn lawyer let that damn, spoiled child make a fool of me."

"Who?" Gail asked.

"Ashley," Sophie hissed. "The bad seed."

"I'm sure we can—"

"Don't you dare," Sophie snapped. "Just find out where she is."

"Ashley?"

"Of course. Who else?"

Gail dialed the number she had in her contacts but it went straight to voice mail, no answer. Not wanting to tell Sophie she'd failed, she called Britney next.

"Gail?" Britney answered. "Is my mom okay?"

"She's fine," Gail said. "Well, she's your mom, so..."

"So she's probably having a fit because I'm not there."

"Something like that."

Britney chuckled. "What's up? Or did you call to vent?"

"We're actually wondering where Ashley is."

"Did she seriously think Ashley would attend?"

"No."

"Then why does she want to know where Ashley is?"

Gail, worried about disappointing Sophie, said, "I think just to ask her something about her father."

Britney was quiet for a moment. "She went to pick up some things at her place but I think she was going to talk to her mother first."

"Talk to her mother?"

"At the cemetery."

# # # #

Sophie dialed Britney's number while she waited for the car. It went to voice mail, so she hung up and dialed again, tapping the numbers hard enough to crack the screen.

"Yes, Mother?" Britney asked.

"Why aren't you here?"

"I'm sorry but I can't do another memorial. I'm not sure I'd even know the people who came."

"He was your stepfather."

"I know."

As Clyde pulled up with the Cadillac, Sophie turned her back, walking along the sidewalk. "You don't think I know what you're doing?"

"What?" Britney asked.

"You're choosing that pathetic fool, Ashley. You think you can get my goat, but I won't stand for it."

"Mother, please."

"I'm cutting you off," Sophie hissed.

Britney sighed.

"You don't care? Fine. Come Monday, Beckley will

rewrite my will."

"That's fine."

"Fine? You don't care about me? You don't care!"

"I'm too sad and tired to discuss it. I'm sorry I couldn't come today, but do what you have to do."

"You're God damn right I'll do what I have to do," Sophie said. "That little bitch is going to find out what happens when you double-cross me."

She hung up.

Sophie panted and squeezed the phone, the heat spreading from her neck to her face and then back down across her chest.

BRITNEY

BRITNEY HAD BEEN IN A STORE on Liberty when her mother called. At first, she'd continued shopping. Angry calls from Sophie were not a new thing.

But the threat had confused her. Staring at the rack of blouses in dark green and orange patterns, she couldn't make sense of what they were, and hurried from the store.

It was bright out but the sun was low enough to be blocked by some of the buildings. A warm breeze full of the scent of grass, earth, and some flowers swept past, turning her to the east. Ashley was somewhere off in that direction, ten or so miles away, unaware that Sophie was approaching.

What would her mother do, anyway? Yell at Ashley? Threaten to sue? Sophie already had all the material possessions.

Britney dialed Ashley's phone number but it went immediately to voice mail, so she was probably at the cemetery.

The light at the corner turned green and the traffic surged along Liberty. Britney crossed the road, picturing what Ashley might be doing at that moment, standing in front of the graves, or maybe kneeling to pull weeds or adjust the flowers. Ashley had invited her but Britney declined, wanting to shop, as if that would make her feel better. What had she been thinking?

As she approached the theater, the sidewalk grew crowded and Britney found herself stopped as people moved around her. Her car was at her apartment building, six blocks the other direction. What was she even doing?

There was no way to get there before Sophie arrived. Ashley was just going to have to handle it herself.

Britney turned to go back home and noticed a bird on a raised planting bed in front of the building. Two house finches picked at a plant, gathering stalks and stems.

"Ashley needs help," Britney said. "Go warn her. Please. She's in danger."

The birds flew off.

Britney watched them rise above the buildings and head east.

Snapping out of it, she looked around to see if anyone took note of what she'd done.

SOPHIE

SOPHIE FUMED IN THE PASSENGER SEAT as Clyde drove east on Interstate 94. Those imbeciles had botched the memorial. How hard could it be to get people to show up for a free meal?

What poison had Ashley spread about David's death? It had to have been Ashley and her unhinged ideas, the radicalism, the *anarchy*. Really, it was all David's fault for not dealing with her properly long ago.

The last exit for Ypsilanti flew past and Sophie was reminded of how she hated the ordinariness surrounding them: the discount stores and fast food; the noisy, domestic cars; and the football weekends. As soon as possible, she would relocate to Bloomfield Hills, or Rochester Hills, or maybe just Farmington Hills. Any of the Hills would be better than this.

They slowed down to exit the highway.

"What's the matter?" Sophie asked.

"Ma'am?"

"Why are you slowing down?"

"It's a surface—"

"Go faster, damn it."

As they crossed they main bridge into Ringerton, Clyde slowed to a crawl and stopped behind several cars.

"Now what?"

Clyde lifted his hands from the wheel. "Traffic light is red."

"Go around them."

Clyde steered right, put two wheels over the curb, and continued moving forward, albeit slowly.

"For the love of Pete," Sophie said.

He turned right and was able to accelerate on the empty stretch of road leading to the bridge leading to the cemetery. Sophie pressed down on the handgun in her purse. There was no reason to shoot her but she might need to scare her, if showing up with Clyde wasn't enough. Hopefully, no one else would be there, and Ashley would feel how alone she was in this world. But if she flipped out...

Once again, Clyde slowed the car to a crawl.

Ahead, a coyote stood in the middle of the approach to the bridge; the coyote's eyes glowed greenish-yellow in the glare of the headlights.

Sophie felt hatred for the beast. How dare it stand there, yet another menace to be removed from her life. She thought of shooting it, or maybe Clyde could do that, but they weren't that far from town.

"Run it over," she said.

"Excuse me?"

"Run *it* over."

Clyde obeyed and punched it.

The coyote had just started toward the bridge when it heard a noise approaching. Back along the path, a thing —a big thing—turned and came closer. The big thing stopped and for a moment they considered each other.

Then the thing roared and charged, gaining speed. The coyote ran toward the tall grass on the sloping hill where it could easily hide.

When the coyote broke for the tall grass, Clyde eased off the gas.

"No you idiot," Sophie hollered. "Kill it."

She pressed his knee down on the accelerator and jerked on the wheel.

The XT6 lunged ahead, toward the coyote, off the road.

Clyde swept Sophie's hands away from the steering wheel and his leg. The rear end slid on the sloped gravel and he jerked the wheel to get back on the road.

As the car lurched to the left, he jerked the wheel back the other way. It lurched even harder to the right, lifting both of them a few inches from the seat. Clyde gripped the steering wheel and stabbed at the brakes, but his foot punched the accelerator by mistake and they sped across the lane, launching the XT6 off the road.

Sophie saw the water ahead but, as the nose tipped forward, the grass and rocks leading to the shore came into view.

The nose of the XT6 slammed into the packed earth embankment thirty feet below. Clyde and Sophie were knocked unconscious by the blast of the airbags.

The XT6 cartwheeled over and the rear end crashed into the stones along the shore. It belly-flopped into the lake and floated out a few feet, into deeper water, and sank.

The onboard concierge connected, and the operator

asked if everyone was okay. "Help is on the way," the operator said.

Sophie came to when the water was up to her chest, the air in the cabin escaping through cracks in the windows. She shouted for help. The operator said, "Ma'am —" but the electrical system shorted and the call dropped.

Up on the road, the coyote watched as the big, noisy thing sank into the water. In the dwindling light, the water was dark, like night. The thing slipped beneath the surface, which churned for a few seconds. Soon, there was nothing more to see. The coyote looked both ways. Convinced no other things were coming, it made its way across the bridge over the lake.

ASHLEY

THE SUN HAD PRETTY MUCH SET, and I was a bit anxious to leave the cemetery. I didn't like staying there after dark.

But the sunset had been lovely, and I felt my mother wanted me to stay near.

A few moments after the shadows fell across the water, I heard some kind of commotion on the bridge. Then I felt relaxed, and I knew my mother and father were fine with me leaving.

As I drove back to the entrance, a coyote trotted along the dirt road. I watched as it made its way into the wooded area and disappeared into the shadows.

38

ASHLEY

I WAS WALKING IN DEPOT TOWN at the beginning of August, vibing on the warm weather, when I saw a help-wanted sign in the window of what used to be Britney's coffee shop. Inside, the shop had the same layout. There was fresh paint and new tables and chairs. The espresso machine was the same one from when I worked there. I could just barely make out the bullet holes in the ceiling.

"Welcome," the woman behind the counter said. "What can I get you?"

"Cappuccino."

When she handed me the drink, I mentioned I used to work there.

"Would you like a job?"

"Not really," I said. "Do you need help?"

She wiped the counter, I think to gather strength, because she hadn't spilled. "I didn't realize how hard it would be to open, close, and do everything else in between."

"It's just you?"

"My husband and I, but we haven't been able to hire anyone yet."

"Probably once the students are back."

I held out my money, but she shook her head. "First one is free."

She seemed nice, and I was happy that there would be coffee here for the neighborhood. "I'll open for you until you hire someone, then train them. Okay?"

"Oh my God, you're an angel!"

I was staying with Britney in her Ann Arbor condo, so it wasn't all that convenient to get to Depot Town that early. I started going over to Kirsten's and Julie's place after my shift, hanging out and napping on their couch like I lived there. No one seemed to mind.

It got me thinking about what I was going to do next.

Were Britney and I going to live together and get old like spinster sisters? Or would one of us tire of the other and pick a fight?

Not likely. We were both getting over some pretty serious shit, going to therapy.

Every night, we'd watch some goofy television show or a movie, things we'd never done before. She'd always been on a wildly serious tennis trajectory all the way through college. I'd hidden in my room and then ran away.

Staring at the television with Britney beside me on the sofa was better than therapy. For the first time, it felt like family.

Britney came home one evening with the news. "Dad's

company is doing okay."

"What does that mean?"

"We got back all the engineers who quit. They picked their own manager. They wanted a pizza oven, so we got them a pizza oven."

"Cool." I had asked little about it since Dad died. In my mind, it was still Sophie's business. That Britney inherited the company, the mansion, and a small fortune was her business.

"George recruited a finance person," she said. "A woman—kind of looks like Sophie, which is weird—and she's working out fine. Beckley, the lawyer, helped track down all the money Frank stole, and that infusion of cash bought us time to rebuild the sales pipeline."

"Great."

"Don't tune out," Britney said. "I feel you're barely listening."

"I'm listening, and I'm happy for you."

Britney put a hand on my head, but in a nice way. "You risked prison for that company."

"I didn't want it for myself. It's fine."

"Do you want to hear any more about it?"

"I'm thinking about what I want to do next," I said. "I may move in with Kirsten and Julie. Maybe go back to school."

"That's great," Britney said. "You can stay here as long as you want."

"I don't want to leave you, and we can still hang out, but I think I missed something by not spending more time with my friends."

Britney leaned across the sofa and hugged me.

"There's one problem."

"Okay."

"I'm going to give the company to you."

"What do you mean?"

"Dad's company, HD Enterprises. I'm going to hand it over to you."

I pointed at the urn holding Sophie's remains. "Is that what she wanted?"

Britney grabbed the scarf we kept handy and draped it over the urn. "You know she was pissed at me about Dad. She totally didn't want me to have it, but she didn't have time to change her will. So I'm giving it to you."

"But I'll just give it away."

"That's fine. I'll help you."

"For real?"

Britney nodded. "Someone's interested in buying the mansion, so I'm going to give most of that money to you, plus a bunch of other stuff. George is almost done with probate."

"I don't want a bunch of money."

"So put it into the business and then give it to the employees, just like you wanted."

The next day, I told the coffee shop owners I was quitting. I had stayed on longer than I expected and had been giving my salary to the other baristas in the tip jar. But they were all going to be fine.

At the end of my shift, as I wrapped up my apron for the last time, the owner came up to me smiling.

"Do you have to leave right away?" she asked.

"No."

"Good. Have a seat."

A guy came in carrying a cake. It was from the vegan bakery down the street. The coffee shop owners and the baristas there gathered around and sang "For She's a Jolly Good Fellow" to me. The cake guy lingered in the back, glancing at me. It was weird, but nice.

Also, the cake was fantastic.

"Are you going back to school or something?" the guy who delivered the cake asked.

"No, I have this other thing to take care of because my dad died."

"Oh God I'm sorry," he said.

He seemed pained, and I felt dumb for saying it like that, making him feel bad. "It's fine," I said. "I mean, it sucks, and I'm miserable, but we're figuring it out."

"Then I'm sorry for your loss."

"My mom died too," I blurted out. I don't know why I said it like that except maybe I didn't want him to ask about her too and feel bad about that.

Sadness spread over his face. "I'm so sorry."

I laughed. "It's okay. Maybe we should start over."

He nodded. "I'm Leon."

"I'm Ashley."

"Nice to meet you."

"Do you go to school at Eastern?"

"I'm taking the semester off, but I'll start again in winter."

"I think that's when I'll start there, too."

"Maybe we can hang out or something."

"Sure."

Over at HD Enterprises, Britney was the boss, and I worked on the plan to give the company to the employees.

It's a complicated thing to give away something like that, and lots of details had to be worked out, like the share of equity each current and former employee would get. We hired a lawyer who had done this before, and he and George did the heavy lifting of writing up the contracts and stuff.

Once word got around, a bunch of former employees came back.

The whole thing was cool and made me happy, but it was also bittersweet. Working on the deal helped me focus, and continuing with therapy helped me in the quiet times.

And when those didn't help, I visited Mom and Dad in the cemetery.

Two months later, a new management team was in place and Britney and I became figureheads, dropping by during the week to bring donuts.

After one of those visits, Britney and I were going to hang at her place and watch a movie, but I asked for a detour. I felt an urge to visit my parents.

The cemetery was cold and barren. The sun was low in the sky and peeked out behind gray clouds. But being there made me happy.

After we tidied up the graves, Britney said, "Do you need some time to talk?"

"I guess not."

We watched a dozen geese flying in formation, honking, I guess, to encourage each other.

"Will you help me plan a memorial and deal with Sophie's remains?" Britney asked.

"Are you dropping her in the ocean?"

Britney scowled. "Is that you or Joan saying that?"

I covered my face while considering the question. "A little of both."

"I'm going to bury her with my father in Farmington Hills."

"Of course I'll help you," I said. "You're my sister."

Besides, I thought it was important to put Sophie six feet under and try to get busy doing something good in the world.

I know that's what my mother wanted for me.

Acknowledgments

This story has evolved over many years and I am indebted to early feedback from Kathryn, Jess and Maddy for steering the ship away from the rocks.

More recently, without feedback from Brian Wallace and Shelly Willoughby, this story would be stinking up the place.

Big shout out to Leon Toomey for a careful read during polish, and to my wife, Mary, for attention to detail pre-launch.

About the Author

Mickey is a Michigan-based writer of suspense, sci-fi and satire. An inveterate storyteller, he's taken the stage at The Moth in Ann Arbor twenty times. He loves to play euchre, Galaxian, and pickleball. Oh, and he can assemble a tent in three minutes.

He lives with his wife, some dogs, and a cat. He spends time with his adult kids as often as possible.

He also thinks he's funny. To judge for yourself, sign up for his newsletter, The Mickey Picayune, at:

www.MickeyHadick.com

Leave a Review

I love that you read my story. I'd love it even more if you left a review somewhere, even a bathroom stall wall. Reviews are the magic elixir that help books sell. If you enjoyed this book, leaving a review would be much appreciated.

Not sure how to write a review?

The review can be a single statement, a paragraph, or a full-blown celebration (but no plot-spoilers!). Just describing who might enjoy it and what you liked can help others understand if the story is a good fit for their tastes.

If you want to let me know what you thought of the story, or to let me know about a review, email me at:

Mick@MickeyHadick.com.